The Beauty with Poison 2
——Against the Current

Shuang Chenyue

Published by Great Wall Publishing, 2024.

Table of Contents

Volume Two: Against the Current

Chapter Eleven: Beauty in the Arms

"Mr. Shaw... Mr. Shaw..."

In his hazy consciousness, Timothy heard a voice echoing repeatedly in his ears. There was a pair of hands, gently tracing the contours of his cheeks, then sliding down provocatively, roaming all over his body.

Timothy groggily opened his eyes a sliver, vaguely seeing a blurry figure gazing down at him in the flickering candlelight. He reached out, trying to grasp the indistinct shadow, but his hand waved futilely through the air, catching nothing.

"Where am I...?"

Timothy slowly opened his eyes fully and sat up, immediately feeling a splitting headache. He held his head, dazed for a moment as his vision gradually cleared.

He found himself in an unfamiliar, empty room. The dim candlelight flickered in the wind, and when he looked up, he saw an intricately carved window lattice. Outside, the night was deep, and a bright moon hung high in the sky.

Timothy tried to recall why he was here. He stood up, walked to the window, and looked out. He saw a river; on this side, the lights were bright, the drums and music were loud, and the streets were bustling with people. On the other side, it was pitch dark, desolate, and filled with cries of misery.

His mind suddenly cleared, and he remembered. This was the administrative center of Sunder—Rickie.

His thoughts took him back to a few hours earlier, when he was walking on the street across the river. After a long journey, Timothy had finally arrived in Sunder from Poiema. Sunder had just experienced a drought, and millions of starving people had flocked to Rickie, the largest city. From the city gates to the heart of Lower River District, corpses littered the roads, and the starving, clothed in rags, lived on the streets. The air was filled with the stench of rot, and garbage piled high.

However, across the river, the Upper River District presented a completely different scene.

The River Filat divided Rickie into two worlds: one of opulence and one of destitution. On one side, the wealthy and powerful lived in luxury, oblivious to the suffering just across the water. The most famous place in Upper River District was Pavilion Lainey, known for its nightly Mable Banquet. As a hub for the local elite, many considered it an honor to attend. Even the newly arrived Timothy had heard of its fame. The King of Nixie, whom Timothy was supposed to visit, was a regular at these banquets.

It seemed he would have to visit Pavilion Lainey himself, Timothy thought.

However, crossing from Lower River District to Upper River District was no easy task. The only way across was the grand structure of Rainbow Bridge. To prevent the impoverished from Lower River District from causing trouble, strict checkpoints had been set up on the bridge. Entry required proof of identity and a pass; without these, entry was forbidden.

When Timothy reached Rainbow Bridge, he was stopped by the officers at the checkpoint, who demanded proof of his identity.

"I am Palace Manager Timothy, an official of the court."

Timothy was carrying a royal decree, so he was confident.

But the officer remained unmoved, "Palace Manager? Never heard of it. If you're a court official, show your decree."

"Of course, I have it. Wait here." Timothy reached for his waist, only to find that his pouch was missing. Cold sweat broke out on his forehead as he realized that his pouch, containing all his money, his royal pass, and important documents, was gone.

"Where is my decree!?"

Panicked, Timothy searched frantically, knowing that losing the documents could lead to severe punishment.

The officer laughed at Timothy's distress, "Stop acting. I've seen plenty like you, thinking they can bluff their way through. Go home and sleep."

He shoved Timothy aside.

"Wait! I really am a court official!!" Timothy protested. "My pass was stolen! Take me to see the King of Nixie! He knows me and will confirm I'm not lying!"

"You think you can see the King of Nixie?" The officer drew his sword, pointing it at Timothy, "Leave now, or I'll send you to hell!"

Knowing these officers were bullies, Timothy didn't back down. He pointed at them and shouted, "You dogs! You look down on people? You think I'm scared of you? I demand to see the King of Nixie! Kill me if you want, but only after I've seen him! If I'm lying, I'll cut off my own head and give it to you!"

"Get him, boys!" The officer yelled, and the other officers swarmed Timothy, pinning him to the ground.

But Timothy fought back, shouting, "Help! These traitors are murdering a court official in broad daylight!!"

The bridge was already crowded with people desperate to enter Upper River District. Hearing Timothy's cries, the crowd surged forward, overwhelming the checkpoint.

The officers panicked, drawing their weapons to fend off the crowd, and in the chaos, they forgot about Timothy. He managed to crawl to the side of the bridge.

Among the desperate crowd were many who had nothing to lose. Facing death every day, they were not afraid of the soldiers' weapons. The bridge descended into chaos, with shouts and screams filling the air. Soon, the checkpoint was overrun, and the masses poured into Upper River District.

Timothy was among them.

As the chaos spilled into the Upper River District, guards were dispatched to quell the disturbance. Armed with swords and shields, they slashed at the intruders, and blood flowed freely.

Timothy, the cause of the chaos—though he didn't see it that way—escaped the slaughter by clambering onto rooftops, leaping between buildings.

In the midst of this turmoil, a procession slowly approached from the distance.

At the center of the procession was a luxurious sedan, carried by attendants. Those who saw it quickly moved aside, some even kneeling in reverence.

"Stop." A cold, melodious male voice commanded from within the sedan.

The procession halted, and an elderly man, dressed as a steward, hurried forward, bowing at the curtain, "What are your orders, young master?"

"What's happening up ahead?"

"Please wait a moment, young master." The steward turned to a guard, "Go see what's going on ahead."

At that moment, a ragged man burst from the chaos, dragging a woman with a baby in her arms. A soldier with a spear chased after them.

"Stop!!"

The couple fled, knocking over several stalls in their path, causing havoc.

"Young master! There's serious trouble up ahead; we need to turn back!" The steward urged.

"Don't panic."

The person inside the sedan chair remained unhurried. As soon as he finished speaking, a slender hand extended from the sedan, gently lifting the curtain. He stepped out slowly.

Timothy was stunned at the sight. The man emerging from the sedan was dressed in a crimson robe embroidered with cloud patterns, a dark silk collar, and wide-sleeved long robes. His long hair cascaded down to his waist, loosely tied with a thin scarlet silk ribbon.

Complementing his noble demeanor was his handsome and delicate appearance, as radiant as the summer sun. From afar, he resembled a jade tree standing tall amidst the clouds, exuding a majestic presence.

Meanwhile, a scream echoed from the front. A man, who had been dragging a woman and running towards them, was struck in the back by a thrown spear. With a groan, he fell to the ground. The woman, terrified, shook her husband's body desperately, but he did not respond. As the officers closed in, she clutched her baby tightly and ran towards the crimson-robed gentleman's entourage.

"Young master! Save us, young master!"

The woman struggled to break through the guards, her baby's cries piercing the air.

The crimson-robed gentleman, however, nonchalantly opened an ivory fan, covering his mouth slightly. His long, phoenix-like eyes narrowed, a frosty glint in his gaze, showing no intention of helping.

Timothy could no longer stand by. He stood up and shouted furiously, "You bunch of heartless men!"

"Who is it!?" Everyone looked up, their eyes landing on Timothy.

Standing on the rooftop, Timothy announced loudly, "I am Timothy, an official of the court! It was I who allowed the refugees in! If you want to arrest someone, arrest me!"

Timothy's declaration caused an uproar below. Even the crimson-robed gentleman opened his eyes slightly wider, silently scrutinizing Timothy on the roof.

The officers' attention shifted to Timothy. Ignoring the woman, one of them pointed at him angrily, "How dare you incite chaos here! Archers, shoot him down!"

At the command, the archers drew their bows, releasing a volley of arrows.

Despite Timothy's bold words, he was no invincible hero. If he stayed put, he would be riddled with arrows. He quickly ducked, but suddenly slipped. With a loud cry, he tumbled down.

"Move aside—I'm falling!"

With a crash, Timothy landed heavily on someone, the impact echoing loudly.

In that moment, Timothy felt his lips press against something soft.

As the dust settled, Timothy realized he had landed on top of someone. The soft sensation was another person's lips.

Stunned for a moment, Timothy quickly pulled back.

He saw that the person beneath him, disheveled, was none other than the dignified and delicate crimson-robed gentleman. The gentleman's fair skin was dusted with dirt, and his lips, which had just met Timothy's, were as red as blood.

"Uh, I... I'm sor..." Timothy's heart raced, leaving him speechless.

Before Timothy could finish, a sharp pain struck the back of his head. His vision blurred as he collapsed unconscious on the crimson-robed gentleman.

"Young master! Are you alright, young master!!"

The butler, holding a wooden stick, stood behind Timothy, his face filled with panic. The guards hurriedly surrounded them, pulling Timothy off the crimson-robed gentleman.

Frowning, the crimson-robed gentleman clutched his chest, coughed a few times, and spoke in a chilling voice, "Cut off this man's tongue! Beat him to death with sticks!"

"Yes!" The guards responded, ready to drag Timothy away.

"Wait!" the crimson-robed gentleman suddenly ordered sharply.

"Young master...?" The guards and the butler exchanged puzzled looks.

The crimson-robed gentleman stood up, walked over to Timothy, and scrutinized his unconscious form. After a moment of contemplation, his lips curved into a barely noticeable smile. "I've changed my mind. Take this man back to the mansion."

Chapter Twelve: Regret Meeting Too Late

Purple smoke curled, the scent of incense lingering in the air.

"I'm sorry—!!!"

Lying on the large bed with crimson curtains, Timothy jolted awake, shouting as he sat up in shock.

The sound echoed emptily in the quiet room. Timothy stared blankly for a moment, then looked down to find himself covered by a soft and luxurious quilt. As he looked around, he realized he was not on the street but in an unfamiliar chamber.

Timothy touched the still slightly aching back of his head and mumbled to himself, "Where is this?"

He got out of bed and curiously examined his surroundings. The chamber was spacious and bright, with a layer of soft carpet on the floor. One entire wall was filled with antique treasures, and the furnishings were meticulously chosen. The bedding and cushions were made of the finest silk, and the swaying beaded curtains were inlaid with dazzling gems and jewels.

Though Timothy was no stranger to luxury, he had to admit that the opulence of this place surpassed even the emperor's palace.

As he looked around, a voice suddenly came from behind him.

"Are you awake, sir?"

Timothy turned around to see a beautiful woman in red, leaning against the screen with an ivory fan in her hand, leisurely watching him. It was the same crimson-robed gentleman he had encountered at the Mervyn market.

"It's you!?" Timothy exclaimed in surprise. "You, you are..."

"Penelope Morris," the beauty introduced herself. "You were knocked unconscious by my men and left on the street. Do you remember that?"

Timothy was stunned. "So this place is..."

"My humble abode," Penelope replied, walking forward and sitting down at a table. She gestured with her hand, "Mr. Shaw, please have a seat."

Timothy, still confused, sat down opposite Penelope. He watched as Penelope picked up a wine jug, gently poured two cups, and pushed one towards Timothy.

"My servants were rude to you earlier, Mr. Shaw. I apologize on their behalf," Penelope said, raising her cup in the air and downing it in one go.

After finishing the drink, Penelope showed the empty cup to Timothy. Seeing Timothy staring at her, she lowered her eyes and asked with a slight tilt of her head, "Mr. Shaw, is there something on my face?"

"No, nothing!" Timothy snapped out of his daze and hurriedly drank the wine, awkwardly smiling. "I must apologize for earlier..."

Thinking of the moment he accidentally kissed Penelope, the soft touch still lingering on his lips, Timothy blushed furiously.

"I really didn't mean to be rude to Mr. Morris! It was just an accident! Yes, an accident!"

Penelope had been silently observing Timothy. Seeing him so flustered, she couldn't help but laugh, closing her ivory fan with a snap and giggling.

"Mr. Shaw, if I hadn't seen my servants bring you back myself, I would doubt that you are the same person who stood on the roof heroically reprimanding everyone earlier."

Timothy scratched his head in embarrassment. "That was a different situation. I was desperate to save someone, and I wasn't thinking straight. Now that I think about it, I'm quite scared. If I hadn't slipped off the roof, I might have been shot to death. So I must thank Mr. Morris for saving my life."

Penelope laughed even harder. "It wasn't me who saved you, but the broken tile that made you slip."

With their conversation, the atmosphere thawed completely. Penelope inquired about Timothy's identity, and Timothy, seeing no reason to hide his mission, told Penelope how Queen Owen had sent him from Poiema to Sunder as a military supervisor.

As Timothy spoke, Penelope kept refilling his cup. Since Timothy was a year older than Penelope, after a few cups of warm wine, they started addressing each other as brothers.

"So, brother, you came to Rickie to find His Highness the King of Nixie?"

"Yes. But as soon as I arrived in Rickie, all my belongings were stolen," Timothy sighed. "Now I can't attend the Mable Banquet, nor do I know where to find the King of Nixie. Losing money is one thing, but without the royal edict and documents, I can't even think of returning to Poiema."

Penelope stood up and walked to the window, pondering. "If it's the Mable Banquet, I might have a way to get you in."

"What!?" Timothy looked up, hope rekindled in his eyes. "Penelope, do you mean it!?"

"You're looking for the King of Nixie, right?" Penelope turned and smiled at Timothy. "I'm planning to attend the banquet tonight. Why don't you come with me? If we find the King of Nixie, you can prove your identity."

"Great!" Timothy jumped up excitedly, grabbing Penelope's hand. "It's a blessing in disguise that I met you. Penelope, you must be my guardian angel!"

Penelope instinctively took a step back, averting her gaze.

"But the Mable Banquet is a gathering of nobles and elites. Brother, you'd better change your outfit if you want to attend."

"Really?" Timothy looked at his attire. "But I dressed like this in the palace too."

Penelope shook her head. "That's not enough. The Mable Banquet is no ordinary party. If you don't dress well, you might be looked down upon."

With that, Penelope took Timothy's hand. "Follow me, brother."

Penelope led Timothy through several rooms, each as luxurious as the last, until they reached a room filled with exquisite jewelry. Upon entering, a dozen maids in splendid attire bowed to them. One maid pulled a rope, slowly drawing back a carved jade screen to reveal an array of magnificent clothes.

Penelope walked forward, her slender fingers skimming over the garments until she settled on a dark blue robe. She pulled it out and held it against Timothy, nodding. "This one looks good. Change into it."

Timothy was puzzled, but Penelope's order sent the maids swarming around him. Without giving him a chance to speak, they began dressing him. Helpless, Timothy let them do as they pleased. Changing clothes wasn't enough—they also applied makeup and styled his hair. By the time they finished, an entire hour had passed.

Timothy sat up straight, despite his aching back, not daring to move an inch. He sighed, "Do you always go through this before attending a party?"

Penelope, holding an eyebrow brush, carefully drew Timothy's eyebrows. "Whether attending a party or not, dressing up properly is basic etiquette, isn't it?"

"I didn't know before, but now I do. It turns out being a man is harder than being a woman."

Penelope laughed softly. "I'm surprised, brother. You have such a good appearance, yet you don't make the most of it. Are you really willing to blend in with the crowd?"

After finishing his eyebrows, Penelope stepped back, admiring her work with satisfaction.

"How is it?" Timothy asked curiously.

"Why don't you see for yourself?" Penelope led him to a polished bronze mirror and smiled. "Aren't you handsome and dashing?"

"Really?" Timothy stared at his reflection. He wasn't sure about Penelope's taste but felt more comfortable with his usual look. Still, being praised by such a beautiful woman made him a bit shy. "If you say it's good, then it must be."

"But this is not enough," Penelope said.

"There's more?" Timothy sighed, leaning weakly. "Can you tell me all at once?"

Penelope stood behind Timothy, smiling mysteriously at his reflection. "You need to prepare some presentable talents."

"Talents?" Timothy was confused. "You mean like playing musical instruments or painting?"

"Something like that." Penelope nodded.

"But I don't know any of those," Timothy looked at Penelope helplessly. "I'm just a commoner with no skills. What if I'm not prepared?"

Penelope smiled, leaning close to Timothy's ear, whispering, "Then you'll 'die' miserably."

Timothy couldn't help but shiver, raising his head and saying, "I only know how to sing Big Drum Storytelling... Does that count as a talent?"

Penelope seemed a bit surprised. "Of course it counts. You know how to do it?"

Timothy nodded, frowning. "I often listened to it on the streets when I was young, so I picked up a bit, but I'm not very good at it..."

Unexpectedly, Penelope's eyes lit up with interest. She grabbed Timothy's arm and said, "I'd love to hear it! Can you perform a piece right now, brother?"

"Do you really want to hear it?" Timothy suddenly felt a bit embarrassed. He touched his nose, gritted his teeth, and said, "Alright, since Penelope has asked, I will give it a try."

Without delay, Penelope immediately ordered a servant to bring a small drum and two clappers for Timothy. She then pulled over a small stool, sat down at the table, and looked at Timothy with expectant eyes. Timothy, holding the drumstick in one hand and the clappers in the other, cleared his throat and began to sing.

This was a piece Timothy had heard countless times growing up, and he could recite it backward by now. He used to sing a few lines for his neighbors and relatives on a whim, but he was always off-key, and the audience would protest and interrupt him halfway through.

However, this time, Penelope did not interrupt him at all. She listened quietly to Timothy's entire performance of Big Drum Storytelling.

When the last note fell, Timothy let out a long breath, feeling a sense of exhilaration he hadn't felt in a long time.

Clap, clap, clap...

After a long silence, Penelope slowly began to applaud.

Penelope's shoulders shook, and she burst into laughter while clapping.

"Hahaha! This is so interesting, so very interesting!" Penelope clapped vigorously, laughing so hard she couldn't straighten up.

Timothy stared at Penelope in shock. It was the first time someone had given such high praise to his Big Drum Storytelling.

"Really!?" Timothy was so excited he could hardly believe it. "Was my singing... really that entertaining!?"

Penelope laughed until tears streamed down her face, nodding repeatedly. "It was brilliant, brother. Let's perform this at the Mable Banquet tonight!"

Timothy was overjoyed, nearly moved to tears. He put down the drumstick and clappers and hugged Penelope. "Penelope, you're the first person to appreciate my performance like this. Are you really not joking with me!?"

Penelope covered her mouth with the ivory fan, her shoulders shaking with laughter. "I swear..."

Seeing Penelope's reaction, Timothy's confidence soared. He nodded and said, "I knew it! In the past, when I sang this for my neighbors, they said I was torturing their ears. How could that be? I sing very well!"

Penelope, still laughing, agreed, "They don't know how to appreciate it. They can't see how much effort you put into your singing."

Timothy nodded vigorously in agreement, gripping Penelope's shoulders. "You're absolutely right! Penelope, you understand me so well! How fortunate I am to have met a kindred spirit like you. I could die without regrets!"

"I'm really looking forward to tonight," Penelope said with a radiant smile. Behind the half-covered ivory fan, her lips curved into a meaningful smile. "I can't wait any longer."

Chapter Thirteen: The Feast of Prosperity

By the banks of the River Filat at night, the air was cool as water, with festive lights everywhere. Timothy sat in the sedan chair, looking at the dazzling lights outside, feeling as if he were in a dream. If he hadn't seen it with his own eyes, he wouldn't have believed that just a few hours ago, a gruesome massacre had taken place on Rickie's most famous street. Now, the blood and chaos had long been buried under the hustle and bustle, disappearing without a trace.

Tonight, Timothy and Penelope were heading to Pavilion Lainey to attend the legendary Mable Banquet.

As soon as Penelope's sedan appeared in front of Pavilion Lainey, a commotion erupted in the crowd.

"Look, Mr. Morris is here!"

"Wow! It's Mr. Morris!!"

Amidst the exclamations of men and women, Penelope stepped out of the sedan with an air of indifference and personally lifted the curtain for Timothy. As Penelope took Timothy's hand and they appeared in front of Pavilion Lainey, they instantly attracted everyone's attention, making a grand entrance under the gaze of the crowd.

"Hey!? Who's that beside Mr. Morris? I've never seen him before."

"Oh my, Mr. Morris is holding his hand!"

"Although I don't know who he is, he's quite handsome..."

Dressed in the splendid clothes Penelope had chosen for him, Timothy felt extremely uncomfortable under the scrutiny and comments of the onlookers, embarrassed to the point of wanting to find a hole to hide in.

"Brother, you're walking out of sync," Penelope glanced at him.

"Uh, really?" Timothy cleared his throat, straightened his back, leaned closer to Penelope, and whispered with a serious expression, "Do I look strange? Why is everyone staring at me? What are they talking about?"

Penelope laughed. "It's because you're good-looking, brother."

Timothy was skeptical. "Really? I thought I wore my clothes inside out."

"You'll get used to it. Don't mind others' gazes," Penelope said, pulling Timothy's hand as they gracefully entered Pavilion Lainey.

Upon entering Pavilion Lainey, Timothy held his breath. The hanging lamps and candles illuminated the three-story interior with splendor. The intersecting beams were adorned with exquisite carvings and beautiful murals. In the center of the hall stood a high platform, draped with flowing red silk from the beams, creating a dreamlike and radiant scene under the shimmering candlelight.

Aside from the central hall on the first floor, there were private rooms of various sizes around each level. Standing by the windows of these rooms, one could overlook the entirety of Rickie at night.

When Timothy arrived, the Mable Banquet had just begun. Amidst the melodious music, servants carried delicious dishes to the tables, while the nobles gathered in small groups, laughing and toasting, creating a lively atmosphere.

Is such a luxurious banquet held every night? Timothy couldn't help but marvel at the extravagance and indulgence of the wealthy.

From the moment they entered, Penelope and Timothy were approached and greeted countless times. Many people came specifically to see Penelope, who seemed to be a prominent figure in Rickie, always surrounded by admirers wherever she went.

Seeing Penelope conversing with these elegantly dressed nobles, Timothy couldn't help but wonder what kind of luck had brought him here. Just on his first day in Rickie, he had already formed a connection with someone as influential as Penelope.

As Timothy stood there daydreaming, Penelope quietly approached him. "Brother, look over there. That's the King of Nixie you're looking for."

Following Penelope's gaze, Timothy saw a man sitting in a corner room, drinking and chatting with a few friends. As Timothy curiously observed him, the King of Nixie seemed to notice their gaze and turned his head, their eyes meeting. Timothy couldn't help but be startled.

How similar!

The King of Nixie looked remarkably like Christopher, especially his eyes, which were almost identical. However, unlike Christopher, the King of Nixie was clearly older, at least in his forties, with a trace of weariness in his sharp features.

"Isn't that Penelope?" The King of Nixie exclaimed upon seeing her, slapping his thigh and striding towards them.

"Your Highness, it has been a while. You are still as spirited as ever," Penelope greeted with a bow and a slight smile.

"And you are still as charming as ever, Penelope!" The King of Nixie laughed heartily, patting her shoulder.

Penelope introduced Timothy to the King of Nixie, "Your Highness, do you recognize this gentleman?"

"I have noticed," the King of Nixie said thoughtfully, "From the moment this young man entered, he has been staring at me. Could he be an acquaintance?"

Timothy quickly knelt before the King of Nixie and said loudly, "I am Timothy, sent by Queen Owen to assume the role of military supervisor in Sunder, here to assist Your Highness!"

"You are Timothy!?" The King of Nixie exclaimed, hurriedly helping Timothy up. "I have heard so much about you, Timothy. I have been eagerly awaiting your arrival!"

Timothy breathed a sigh of relief. "So the Queen has already informed Your Highness. Before coming here, I was worried that if Your Highness didn't recognize me and I had no proof of my identity, it would be quite embarrassing. Haha..."

"The Queen?" The King of Nixie shook his head with a smile. "No, it wasn't the Queen."

Timothy was taken aback. "Uh? Then who...?"

The King of Nixie leaned close to Timothy's ear and whispered, "The Emperor."

Timothy's eyes widened, his heart racing. "The Emperor... he mentioned me? What did he say?"

The King of Nixie downed his wine in one gulp, looking at Timothy with a smile but saying nothing.

"Your Highness, please don't look at me like that. It's unsettling!" Timothy said, feeling a bit uneasy.

"Don't worry about the details. Come, let's have a drink together! Timothy, or rather, Mr. Shaw."

Before Timothy could respond, the King of Nixie wrapped an arm around his shoulder and led him to the private room, introducing him to his friends. Upon hearing that Timothy was a favorite of Queen Owen, the others eagerly warmed up to him, showering him with enthusiasm.

Just then, a loud drumbeat echoed through the pavilion, followed by the sudden dimming of the candles, leaving only a red lantern on the high platform. In the flickering light, a figure holding a sword appeared faintly behind the swaying red silk.

Timothy was puzzled when he heard someone nearby whisper, "Look, it's Penelope's turn to perform."

(What!? Penelope!?)

Timothy was surprised, only now realizing that Penelope had disappeared from his side.

"This is a tradition at the Mable Banquet," the King of Nixie whispered to Timothy. "Everyone must perform a talent. Only if everyone acknowledges your talent do you pass; otherwise, you have to drink as a forfeit."

So this was the talent performance Penelope had mentioned, the one that would result in a miserable outcome if unprepared? It turned out that even Penelope couldn't escape this so-called tradition.

Timothy looked towards the stage. With a sound of the zither, Penelope raised her hand, and the soft sword in her hand flashed like lightning, darting out like a swimming dragon. With a light tap of her toes, she jumped onto several drums placed on the high platform, gracefully leaping into the air. With the rhythmic and dynamic drumbeats, she danced effortlessly between the drums, her red sleeves fluttering like fire, her belt flowing like a celestial being.

"I never imagined he had such talent..."

Timothy watched the red figure on the stage in a daze, unable to find a word other than "beautiful" to describe what he saw.

The King of Nixie leaned over again. "Penelope's sword dance is arguably the best in Great Alvah. It's not something you can see just anywhere. You're in for a treat tonight."

As the King of Nixie said, the audience was as captivated as Timothy, mesmerized by Penelope's exquisite dance. Cheers, applause, and shouts of admiration filled the hall, everyone's eyes glued to the enchanting figure on the high platform.

"How is it? Isn't it breathtaking?" The King of Nixie asked with a smile.

"It's so beautiful... indescribably beautiful..." Timothy watched without blinking, completely mesmerized.

"But this isn't the most captivating part of the performance. The best part is yet to come," the King of Nixie said, smiling mysteriously.

Before the King of Nixie finished speaking, Penelope leapt into the air, catching hold of a crimson ribbon hanging from the beams. Swinging around the high platform like a soaring phoenix, she dazzled the audience. At the same time, Penelope boldly removed a fine white jade pendant from her neck and tossed it into the air. The pendant traced a graceful arc before landing among the spectators, who clamored to catch it.

Timothy watched in awe as the King of Nixie explained with a smile, "This is Penelope's habit. Every time he performs a sword dance, he throws various priceless jewelry and ornaments into the crowd as gifts."

As the red figure swung closer, Timothy felt Penelope glance at him. Suddenly, something was thrown his way, and he instinctively reached out to catch it. When he opened his hand, he found Penelope's ivory fan.

His heart skipped a beat. He brought the fan to his nose and caught a faint whiff of Penelope's subtle fragrance.

When Timothy looked up again, Penelope had landed on the platform. What followed was even more astonishing. Penelope, appearing intoxicated, began to undress, revealing his pale skin glistening with sweat. He discarded his clothes piece by piece, his muscular, toned body gradually exposed, all under the dim lighting and the veil of thin silk.

"What is he doing!?" Timothy exclaimed, standing up in alarm.

"Don't worry, the best part is yet to come," the King of Nixie replied, leisurely sipping his wine.

Penelope continued stripping, almost entirely naked now. His chiseled muscles and taut waist were clearly defined, his rounded buttocks leading to long, slender legs. If it weren't for the dim light and the thin veil, his private parts would have been exposed to all.

"Your Highness! This, this..." Timothy was red-faced and sweating. "Why isn't anyone stopping him!?"

"I told you, it's part of the performance," the King of Nixie said with a half-smile.

"This counts as a performance!?"

Looking around, Timothy saw that not only was Penelope unfazed, but the audience was also cheering wildly. Some even began to mimic him, stripping off their own clothes in excitement. Timothy felt his whole world crumbling. The decadence and promiscuity of the nobles were a stark contrast to his innocent and straightforward nature.

When Penelope finished his performance and returned, he had changed into another outfit, looking as elegant as ever.

"Well?" Penelope picked up a glass of wine, approached Timothy, and asked with a smirk, "Brother, did you enjoy my performance?"

Timothy stared into Penelope's still slightly flushed eyes and whispered, "Can I be honest?"

"Of course," Penelope replied, her eyes shimmering.

"You are..." Timothy took a deep breath and said, "A beast in gentleman's clothing."

Penelope was momentarily taken aback before bursting into laughter.

"Well said, I am indeed a beast in gentleman's clothing," Penelope laughed, turning to the crowd. "Everyone, Mr. Shaw here has prepared a special performance for us tonight. What do you think, would you like to see it?"

"Yes!" the crowd roared, "Give us a show, give us a show!"

"Is it my turn now?" Timothy said, resigning himself to fate. Despite losing his confidence after seeing Penelope's explosive performance, he took a deep breath and stood up. "Alright, I'll perform my best piece, the Shaw family Big Drum Storytelling!"

Just like during the day, Timothy held the clappers in one hand and the drumstick in the other, setting up a small drum before him and starting his meticulously prepared performance.

However, when he finished and looked up, he was met with faces as if everyone had eaten something foul.

"Mr. Shaw, is that it?"

"What did you just sing?"

—Unbelievably, the entire hall fell silent. Even the King of Nixie looked awkward. "Mr. Shaw, are you trying to embarrass me? How am I supposed to praise that?"

"Really!? Was my singing that bad!?" Timothy couldn't believe it.

"It was beyond terrible," the King of Nixie replied seriously.

"But Penelope..." Timothy looked towards Penelope, but he just sat there, drinking, completely indifferent.

"Hey! Penelope, didn't you say my Big Drum Storytelling was great!?" Timothy grabbed Penelope's shoulder angrily.

"Did I?" Penelope glanced at him, "Maybe I did? Sorry, I must have said it casually and forgotten."

"You...!" Realizing he had been deceived, Timothy was furious.

"Brother, you lost," Penelope said with a smirk, twisting Timothy's wrist onto the table. "As agreed, the loser drinks."

"That's right!" The King of Nixie placed a large jar of wine before Timothy. "You have to toast everyone here."

Timothy's face turned ashen. He glanced around at the crowd, gritted his teeth, and said, "Fine, I, Timothy, will take my loss. I'll toast everyone here!"

"Wait," Penelope stopped him. "Who said it was just everyone here?"

Standing up, he waved his sleeve and pointed to the entire hall. "It's everyone in Pavilion Lainey. One cup each."

"What—!?"

A bolt from the blue, Timothy's mind went blank.

That night, Timothy didn't remember how he toasted. He only remembered that halfway through, he was already drunk, full of anger and frustration, slumping onto Penelope, protesting loudly. Eventually, he passed out in Penelope's arms, unconscious.

In the dead of night, Timothy felt hands roaming over his body. Drunk and hazy, he could barely open his eyes, his vision blurred.

"Mr. Shaw..."

The voice, hot and close, was seductive.

"Is it you, Penelope..."

Timothy instinctively reached out, pulling the person closer.

"You... hic... made me suffer..." he mumbled, "But if you say... sorry... hic... I'll forgive you..."

The person in his arms struggled.

"Penelope, what are you doing..." Timothy slurred, "Don't move... or I won't be able to... hic... control myself..."

"..."

Silence followed.

Eventually, Timothy slowly opened his eyes.

"Where... am I...?"

He sat up, his head throbbing. He held his head, disoriented, as his vision cleared.

He found himself in an unfamiliar, empty room. The flickering candlelight cast shadows, and through a delicate carved window, he saw the night sky and a bright moon.

Staggering to the window, he gazed at the moon, recalling his journey to Sunder, meeting Penelope, and attending the Mable Banquet.

"Villain! Die—!"

Suddenly, a cold flash aimed straight at Timothy. Reflexively, he ducked, and a sharp blade brushed past his head. With a crash, a masked figure burst through the window, charging at Timothy with a knife.

Chapter Fourteen: The Lamb to the Slaughter

"Help! Somebody help!"

Timothy's mind cleared instantly as he cried out for help, desperately dodging the attacks.

"Who are you!? Why are you trying to kill me!?"

The dagger in the black-clad man's hand whizzed past Timothy's cheeks and arms, leaving bloody trails. Each time, Timothy narrowly evaded the lethal strikes, with the blade almost hitting vital points several times. Timothy scrambled around the chamber, using his agility to dodge and weave around the pillars, trying to outmaneuver his assailant.

"Wait! Let's talk this out. Whatever you want, just say it. I'll give you anything I can!"

Timothy shouted. The black-clad man clicked his tongue in annoyance, then kicked a stool into the air. With a swift horizontal kick, the stool flew toward Timothy like a projectile. Timothy tried to escape, but he was a step too slow. With a heavy thud, the stool struck the back of his head. Timothy's vision went black, and he collapsed to the ground, unconscious.

In his entire life, Timothy had never been knocked out twice in one day by different people using different weapons. A lesser man might have had his skull split open or been left with permanent damage. But somehow, Timothy survived with nothing more than a swollen bump on the back of his head.

However, Timothy questioned whether this could be considered luck. Not only had he been robbed of all his belongings on his first day in Rickie, but he was also now tied up and thrown into

an unfamiliar hall, surrounded by a gang of fierce-looking bandits, looking every bit like a lamb awaiting slaughter.

Timothy sat helplessly among the bandits, trembling as he spoke.

"Um, can someone tell me what's going on?"

"You said your name is Timothy?"

A clear voice suddenly called out from the hall. Timothy looked
toward the source and saw a young man sitting nonchalantly in
the main seat to the east. This was the person who had spoken.

Timothy examined the young man closely. Despite his rough attire, the youth had a refined and handsome appearance. He sat in
a chair covered with white tiger fur, one leg crossed over the other, supporting his chin with one hand, lazily observing Timothy.

"The Chief Master is talking to you! Why are you just staring?"

A black-clad man barked angrily at Timothy. When Timothy
turned to look, he was startled.

"You... you're the one who tried to kill me last night!"

"Chief Master, don't listen to this nonsense! He is Penelope! I,
Harley Price, can vouch for it!"

"Wait!" Timothy couldn't bear it anymore. "Which of your eyes
sees that I'm Penelope?? Do I have 'Penelope' written on my forehead?? I get it, you're an assassin, hired to kill someone, right?
Please, look clearly and make sure you're targeting the right person!"

"If you say you're not Penelope, how can you prove it?"

At that moment, a scholarly-looking man with a refined face and
a neatly groomed mustache spoke from the crowd.

"I..." Timothy was momentarily taken aback. "I'll be honest with
you. I'm an outsider. Anything that could prove my identity was
stolen on my first day in Rickie. I'm penniless and don't know
anyone here. If you insist I'm Penelope, I can't prove otherwise.
But think about it, if someone as wealthy as Penelope were kid-
napped, his family would surely notice. Within three days, they

would send someone with a large ransom. Isn't that why you captured Penelope in the first place? For money? Just wait and see. In three days, if no one comes with money to ransom me, you'll know I'm not Penelope."

"Nonsense! Do you think I captured you for money!?" Harley shouted.

"Not for money?" Timothy was puzzled. "Then why? You can't possibly want to make me the chieftain's wife, can you?" He glanced at the Chief Master with his peripheral vision.

"Are you truly foolish or just pretending?" The scholar sneered. "Do you know the reputation of Sabra Village in Sunder?"

Sabra Village?

Timothy's heart skipped a beat. He had indeed heard of many bandit strongholds in the Sunder area during his journey from Poiema. Due to natural disasters and wars, many refugees banded together under capable leaders, occupying mountains and developing their own armed forces. Some powerful factions operated independently, posing a significant threat to the local authorities.

Perhaps Sabra Village was one of the rebellious forces the King of Nixie had mentioned.

The scholar continued, "Many people want to join Sabra Village, but the rule is that they must assassinate or capture a corrupt official or merchant as an Oath of Allegiance. Penelope is one of those targets."

"Oh... I get it now. So you tried to join Sabra Village but captured the wrong person!" Timothy shook his head at Harley. "It's a pity I'm not Penelope. Even if you cut off my head, it won't help you."

Harley, frustrated, retorted, "Stop denying it! If you're not Penelope, why are you wearing his clothes!?"

"He lent them to me."

"Then why were you in his bed?"

"I got drunk, and he took me to his room."

"And this fan!?" Harley stepped forward, holding up Penelope's ivory fan. "This fan is Penelope's beloved possession, never leaving his side. How did it end up with you!?"

"I... picked it up..."

"Nonsense! Such a coincidence doesn't exist!"

"I..."

Timothy was speechless. It dawned on him how suspicious the situation looked. Why did all the incriminating evidence point directly at him? The clothes were chosen by Penelope. The fan was thrown to him by Penelope. He ended up in Penelope's room because he was tricked and got drunk at Pavilion Lainey.

Was it really just a coincidence?

"Could it be..." Timothy's mind reeled, struck by a sudden realization. "I was set up by Penelope?"

"Don't tell us Penelope framed you as a scapegoat?" The scholar said coldly. "Do you think we would believe that?"

"I wouldn't believe it either if I hadn't experienced it myself!" Timothy felt a surge of anger and frustration, slamming his fist on the ground. "Damn you, Penelope! So this was your plan all along! I, Timothy, was so foolish to fall for it!"

"Quite a performance," Harley said dismissively. "Chief Master, whether he's Penelope or not, he's definitely associated with him. He's no good. We should kill him!"

"Associated!?" Timothy's face turned red with anger as he defended himself. "That's not true! I have no connection with Morris! We're not even friends! Chief Master, I'm truly innocent!"

"Silence."

The Chief Master commanded, and the hall fell silent. He had listened quietly for a long time and now stood up, walking slowly to Timothy. With the hilt of his sword, he lifted Timothy's chin.

"If you claim not to be Penelope, you have three days to prove it. If you are an innocent civilian, Sabra Village will not trouble you. But if we find out you are an agent of the authorities..."

Timothy met the Chief Master's sharp gaze and swallowed nervously. "And if I am an agent?"

The Chief Master's eyes darkened. "Then we'll chop you up and feed you to the dogs."

Life is full of unexpected "surprises." One day Timothy was toasting with nobles at Pavilion Lainey; the next, he found himself a prisoner in a bandit's lair.

And it was all thanks to one person.

"I must have been blind!"

Timothy held a straw man in his hand, punching its face. Still unsatisfied, he threw it to the ground and stomped on it several times.

After being thrown into Sabra Village's dungeon, the bored Timothy wove a small straw man from the scattered hay on the ground. He bit his finger and used his blood to write "Morris" on the straw figure.

"Morris, you better pray that I, Timothy, never see you again. If I survive this, I will make sure you regret it!"

"Who are you planning to make regret it?" A voice came from the entrance of the dungeon.

Timothy looked up to see a young boy standing outside the cell, arms crossed, leisurely observing him. Behind the boy stood two burly men, one with a full beard and the other with a face so dark it shone, indicating he was a Dunn Slave.

The boy had wild hair tied into a high ponytail, and his large, sharp eyes glinted with intelligence.

"Who are you?" Timothy asked curiously.

"My name is Adam Garcia." The boy lifted his chin. "The Chief Master sent me to interrogate you."

Timothy asked, "Interrogate me about what?"

"Less talking, follow me."

Timothy followed Adam to a dark, cramped chamber. As soon as Timothy stepped in, his heart sank.

Though small, the chamber was filled with a variety of torture instruments. Stocks, wooden restraints, the tiger bench, and wooden donkey were familiar to Timothy, but there were also many bizarre devices he couldn't name.

Once inside, Timothy was tied to a wooden pillar by the two burly men. In front of him was a grand chair, where Adam sat, legs crossed.

"Speak. What is your relationship with Penelope?" Adam crossed his arms and stared at Timothy. "We've checked, and you're indeed not Penelope. But you are definitely not an ordinary person."

Timothy swallowed. "What exactly did you find out?"

"We're the ones asking the questions!" The bearded man beside Adam barked.

"Just answer my questions obediently. Don't say anything unless I ask." Adam cleared his throat and raised an eyebrow.

Timothy's mind raced. These bandits, enemies of the government, despised both the wealthy and officials. Whether from local or central government, any official would be killed without mercy. It was best to keep his identity hidden and pretend to know nothing.

Adam asked, "Where are you from?"

"Poiema," Timothy answered honestly.

"Poiema?" Adam narrowed his eyes. "Poiema is far from Sunder. Why did you come to this remote place?"

"I... well, I'm a fugitive!"

"A fugitive?" Adam seemed surprised. "What crime did you commit?"

"Well, I couldn't stand corrupt officials!"

Adam stood up and scrutinized Timothy's attire with disdain. "And then you threw yourself into Penelope's bed?"

Timothy, embarrassed, quickly shook his head. "No, no, no! Young Master Adam, you must understand, I had just arrived in Sunder, completely unfamiliar with the place. I heard that Mervyn was home to the rich and powerful, especially the Mable Banquet, which is a social hub for dignitaries. So, I thought I'd sneak into Pavilion Lainey to gather information. But you know, Pavilion Lainey isn't a place just anyone can enter. That's when I met Penelope. He said he could get me in, so I followed him."

"So, you don't know Penelope's true identity?" Adam asked, widening his eyes.

Timothy shook his head. "I really don't. Who is he? Why do you want to kill him?"

"He is the Lord of Sunder, commanding ten thousand troops. His grandfather is Cypress Morris, a founding hero of Great Alvah."

"You mean the general who was a master marksman and saved the founding emperor's life!?" Timothy was stunned. "I never imagined that someone so flamboyant... came from a family of military generals."

Adam observed Timothy's expression closely. "It seems you truly didn't know his background."

"I've been saying that! If I knew, why would I end up as his scapegoat!?"

"Adam, we can't trust his words!" The bearded man beside Adam said. "Remember, we recently executed a spy from the government who had a similar story. Especially since this man has ties with Penelope, he's even more suspicious!"

"Yes, Adam," the Dunn Slave echoed. "After our recent defeats against Sunder's army, there has been an unusual calm. Penelope is known for his cunning. We must be vigilant against his secret plots!"

Adam nodded thoughtfully. "So, what do you suggest we do with him?"

"Isn't it obvious?" The two burly men said in unison, "Torture him!"

"Wait!" Timothy panicked upon hearing the word 'torture'. "I've told you everything. I've been cooperative. What more do you want? Even if you kill me, there's nothing more to say!"

"People always talk big before they've experienced pain." With a snap, Adam cracked a long whip. "Do you know the last person who said that is now lying six feet under?"

As soon as he finished speaking, Adam lashed the whip at Timothy. Reflexively, Timothy turned his face away, expecting searing pain, but the whip didn't hurt as much as he expected.

(He isn't using full force? Why?)

Timothy was puzzled, turning to look at Adam. Adam had a healthy tan, a sign of someone who spent a lot of time outdoors. His thin lips curved slightly, and his large, lively eyes sparkled in the candlelight.

On closer inspection, Adam was quite handsome and rather charming.

Adam whipped Timothy a few more times but, seeing Timothy didn't cry out, he grew frustrated and shouted, "What are you looking at!"

"Ah! Ouch, it hurts!" Timothy suddenly realized and exaggeratedly howled, "I'm going to die!"

Adam, startled by Timothy's reaction, muttered to himself, "Strange, I didn't hit that hard."

Timothy, however, was now fully committed to his act, wailing louder. "Just kill me already! You blind, heartless scoundrels will face retribution for killing the innocent!"

"Retribution..."

Adam hesitated, the whip frozen in mid-air, unsure whether to continue.

By now, Timothy understood. Despite Sabra Village being a bandit's den, not everyone was a ruthless killer. Adam, at least, seemed to have a kind heart.

The problem was Adam's two henchmen.

"Adam, if you can't do it, let us handle it." The bearded man stepped forward, whispering in Adam's ear.

"Yes, the last spy confessed everything in less than half an hour when we interrogated him."

Since earlier, these two had been pushing Adam to torture Timothy, clearly unwilling to let him go easily.

Adam thought for a moment and nodded. "Alright, he's yours. But be careful. We need to keep him alive this time."

"Yes, sir!"

Timothy noticed the eagerness in the henchmen's eyes and shivered. His gaze shifted to the array of torture devices on the walls and floor, a cold sweat breaking out as a sense of dread filled him...

Chapter Fifteen: Beyond Control

After handing Timothy over to his two subordinates, Adam left the dungeon.

As soon as Adam was gone, the bearded man and the Dunn Slave exchanged a knowing, malicious grin.

"Hehe, brother, our chance has come," the Dunn Slave said, rubbing his hands together.

"Indeed, little brother, this one's a prime catch," the bearded man said, licking his lips as he stared at Timothy.

"You... what are you planning to do!?" Timothy felt an unprecedented sense of danger. The way these two hulking men, each a head taller than him, were closing in made him feel like a piece of meat before ravenous wolves.

Seeing the two burly men approaching, Timothy struggled desperately, but his hands and feet were tightly bound to the wooden pillar, making it impossible to break free.

"Gentlemen, let's talk this over. Whatever you want, just say the word. I'll do my best to satisfy you!" Timothy pleaded.

"Anything we want, you say? Shaw, you said it yourself!" the bearded man replied with a sinister smile.

"In that case..." The Dunn Slave pulled a suspicious-looking bottle from his pocket. "Start by drinking this in one go."

Timothy swallowed nervously. "What is that? It's not poison, is it?"

"Of course not," the bearded man said, patting Timothy's face. "A handsome man like you would be wasted if poisoned."

"This is called Death Drink," the Dunn Slave explained, grinning. "After drinking it, you'll feel a burning desire all over. No matter how virtuous or disciplined you are, you'll become as hard as iron, continuously climaxing and ejaculating until you... die from exhaustion."

Timothy turned pale. "No way! That cruel!? Was that what happened to the previous guy...?"

"Indeed," the bearded man chuckled. "After drinking Death Drink, he confessed everything. But he was too weak. Before my brother and I could have enough fun, he passed out and couldn't be revived."

"Both of you... together?" Timothy was horrified. Now it made sense. "You're both... filthy perverts! Drugging prisoners to force them into...?"

"So what if we drug them? So what if we're perverts?" The Dunn Slave snapped, poking Timothy's chest. "A pretty boy like you will never understand our pain!"

"Exactly!!" The bearded man huffed, stamping his foot. "Are you saying we should stay lonely forever, just because of how we look!? Don't we deserve some fun too!?"

Timothy was speechless. If his hands were free, he'd have gouged his own eyes out.

"Brother, let's not waste time talking. Adam might come back any moment."

"True, let's get the drug down him!"

With that, the two men approached Timothy, opening the bottle and forcing it toward his mouth.

"Hey! Let me go!" Timothy turned his head away, shouting, "Help... Help!!"

"Brother, quick! If he keeps shouting, Adam will hear!"

"Drink it!"

They held Timothy's head still, pinching his jaw to force his mouth open. Despite his struggle, Timothy couldn't resist the strength of the two burly men. The liquid poured down his throat.

The hot liquid burned his throat, and as the reality of what was about to happen dawned on him, Timothy was filled with terror. A surge of survival instinct kicked in. Timothy, though not known for his valor, was still an official of the court. If he were to die here in such a humiliating manner, how would history remember him?

"Timothy, on a certain day of a certain month, died in the Sabra Village dungeon, after being drugged and sexually assaulted by two burly men, eventually dying from exhaustion."

—That would be too humiliating!!

Fueled by this thought, Timothy found a burst of strength. He first freed one leg, then lifted his knee and struck the bearded man in the groin.

"Aaah—!" The bearded man screamed, clutching his groin and stumbling back. He fell, writhing in pain, unable to stand. The bottle in his hand shattered on the ground, spilling the remaining Death Drink.

"You...!?" The Dunn Slave was shocked. Before he could react, Timothy freed his other hand, grabbed a nearby torture device, and swung it at his head.

A wooden stock flew through the air, hitting the Dunn Slave squarely on the temple. He collapsed instantly.

In a matter of seconds, the situation had completely reversed.

The bearded man and the Dunn Slave were now tied back-to-back.

"Brother, please, just once, please..." The bearded man, though bound, stared at Timothy's crotch with lustful eyes, swallowing hard.

Timothy looked down. In the heat of the struggle, he hadn't noticed, but now he realized that his crotch had tented, aching with arousal.

"Get lost!" Timothy kicked the bearded man in the groin again. The man screamed, this time with a hint of excitement, "More, brother, harder!"

Just then, a voice called from outside.

"Hey, what's going on in there!?"

Adam had returned, worried about leaving his subordinates alone for too long. He rushed in to find the bearded man and the Dunn Slave bound together, with cloth stuffed in their mouths, whimpering.

"What... happened here!?" Adam ran to them, removing the cloth. "Where's Timothy!?"

"Behind you!" the Dunn Slave groaned.

Adam turned to see Timothy trying to sneak out.

"Stop right there!" Adam kicked the door shut, trapping Timothy inside.

Adam, trained in combat, lashed his whip at Timothy. Timothy, unable to defend himself, could only dodge, his newfound energy from the aphrodisiac giving him an unexpected agility. Despite Adam's relentless pursuit, Timothy remained elusive.

By now, the dungeon was a wreck, most of the torture devices destroyed.

Cornered, Timothy clung to a wooden pillar, his face red, gasping, "If you don't let go, I won't be able to control myself!"

"Stop resisting!" Adam commanded, tightening his grip on the whip. They struggled until, with a ripping sound, Timothy's pants tore, and he was flung against Adam.

"Get off...!" Adam pushed against Timothy, trying to free himself.

"Don't move!" Timothy shouted.

Adam froze, feeling something hard pressing against his waist. He reached down and saw Timothy's engorged member, freed from his torn pants, rubbing against him.

Already on the brink, Timothy finally couldn't hold back. His hips bucked, and he came.

Adam's face turned white. "You... pervert!"

With a scream, Adam kicked Timothy off. Timothy lay on the ground, groaning in pain. "They... drugged... me!"

"What!? Drugged!?" Adam was bewildered. "What happened?"

Turning to the bearded man and the Dunn Slave, Adam saw their guilty expressions and noticed the shattered bottle on the floor.

Realizing the truth, Adam carefully helped Timothy up. "Are you... okay?"

"Do I look like I'm okay?" Timothy was on the verge of tears.

Having been forced to drink more than half the bottle of the drug, Timothy's condition was evident. His swollen member was larger and thicker than usual, its color darker, and it stood rock-hard, leaking clear fluid.

"You two!" Adam supported the panting Timothy, turning angrily to the two men. "Where's the antidote? Give it to me now!"

"Adam... it's an aphrodisiac, there's no antidote..." the bearded man admitted, guilt-ridden. "Unless..."

"Unless what!?"

"Unless you let us relieve him..."

"I'd rather die!" Timothy lay in Adam's arms, his eyes dull. Holding Adam's hand, he said, "Adam, just kill me. Dying in the hands of someone as beautiful as you... wouldn't be the worst way to go..."

"This..." Adam was frantic, like an ant on a hot pan, unsure what to do. Seeing Timothy's growing agony, he hesitantly reached out and wrapped his hand around Timothy's burning shaft.

The moment Timothy felt the cool touch, he looked up in surprise.

Adam's ears were bright red. He turned his face away, unable to meet Timothy's fervent gaze, but his hand began to move, stroking Timothy's throbbing member.

Timothy exhaled heavily. "I knew I wasn't wrong about you, Adam. You really are a good person..."

Adam was taken aback, meeting Timothy's tear-filled eyes.

"But, just using your hand isn't enough." Timothy tugged at Adam's clothes, his eyes pleading. "I need something tighter, hotter..."

"What do you mean by tighter... hotter..." Adam swallowed hard.

"You know what I mean." Timothy's voice dropped to a whisper as he looked into Adam's eyes. "Adam, be a good Samaritan to the end, please."

Adam's face was flushed, and he averted his gaze, looking conflicted.

"If you won't, then just kill me and put me out of my misery," Timothy pleaded.

Perhaps Timothy's earnest plea worked, because after a fierce internal struggle, Adam finally, reluctantly, began to undo his belt.

Timothy, impatient with Adam's slow movements, reached out and yanked his half-removed trousers down. Adam yelped, and before he knew it, his pants were around his ankles, exposing his round buttocks and bare legs to everyone.

"Wait... huh!?" Adam barely had time to react before Timothy, unable to wait any longer, pounced on him.

"Adam, forgive me!"

Timothy inserted a finger into Adam's entrance, prying open the tight passage.

"Ah...!" The intrusion made Adam instinctively close his legs. "It hurts... wait!"

"No time to wait!"

Timothy was relentless. With his shaft painfully swollen and desperate, he barely took time to prepare Adam before positioning himself and pushing the hot, hard tip against Adam's tight opening.

"Adam, I'm going in."

Before Adam could protest, the thick head forced its way inside, pushing deep.

"No..." The pain was overwhelming, and Adam felt like he was being torn apart. "Stop, I can't..."

"It's too late to back out now," Timothy growled, thrusting deeper. "It's already in!"

Adam's body convulsed, tears streaming down his face. He shook his head, kicking and thrashing in a vain attempt to dislodge Timothy. "Don't, please..."

But Timothy, driven to madness by the drug, was beyond reason. He grabbed Adam's ankle, hoisting his leg over his shoulder, and spread Adam's cheeks wide. His cock, fully engulfed, thrust to the hilt.

"Mm...!" Adam's eyes rolled back as his body arched in agony.

"So tight... I'm going to cum!"

The sensation of Adam's tight walls gripping him was electric. Timothy's mind went blank as he climaxed, filling Adam with his seed.

"Stop... stop!" Adam had given up resisting, tears pouring down his cheeks. "Don't move..."

"I can't stop, my body... it's moving on its own..."

Adam couldn't believe Timothy was still hard after cumming twice, but he had no choice but to endure. He clung to Timothy's back, a helpless ship in a storm, tossed about by Timothy's relentless thrusts.

The bearded man and the Dunn Slave watched, envious and jealous, as Timothy's thick, dark member plunged into Adam's filled hole, making obscene squelching sounds.

Timothy, not satisfied, pulled Adam up and continued to pound him from below, lifting him up and down.

Adam, usually a respected figure in Sabra Village, was now spread open, his abused entrance leaking cum as Timothy violated him in front of his subordinates.

But the most humiliating part was his own body. Despite the pain and degradation, Adam's own cock was hard, dripping with precum, a traitorous sign of his arousal.

"Don't look..." Adam shook his head frantically, but his plea only made Timothy thrust harder. Adam's upper body arched back, his head resting on Timothy's shoulder, each thrust pushing his hips forward.

The bearded man and the Dunn Slave watched in awe, their noses bleeding from the intensity.

Timothy wasn't deliberately torturing Adam, but the drug had stripped him of all reason. He could only act like a wild beast, venting his lust on Adam.

"Stop... stop..." Adam cried, his stomach spasming uncontrollably as his own cock twitched and sprayed clear fluid.

"No more..." Adam's cry came too late. Timothy seized his waist and pushed deep, filling Adam with another load of thick cum.

This was Timothy's third orgasm.

Yet he couldn't stop. He knew it wasn't just the aphrodisiac.

Timothy continued to thrust, nibbling on Adam's ear.

"Is it... not over..." Adam's tearful eyes fluttered. "I... can't take it..."

"Just one more time," Timothy said, moving from Adam's ear to his lips. Adam tried to turn away, but met Timothy's gaze. In that moment, an unspoken feeling passed between them, and Adam, trembling, looked away.

"Then... just one more time."

Chapter Sixteen: A Heroic Rescue

Early one morning, Sabra Village Chief Master Abbe Simpson was patrolling the village as usual when he saw someone hurriedly approaching. It was his trusted subordinate, Adam.

Seeing Adam reminded Abbe of the task he had given him a few days ago—to thoroughly investigate Timothy's identity. The three-day deadline had arrived, and Abbe wondered about the progress.

"Adam!"

"Ch-Chief Master!" Adam looked up and quickly saluted, "You're up early today, Chief Master!"

"Where are you coming from?"

Abbe, known for his forthright personality and camaraderie with his subordinates, casually slung an arm around Adam's shoulder, only then noticing the medicine bag Adam was carrying.

"Are you sick?"

"Well... I caught a cold, so I went to see Doctor Cui to get some medicine," Adam said, avoiding eye contact.

"How careless of you. Let me see what medicine you got." Without waiting for a response, Abbe took the medicine bag from Adam's hand and started examining its contents.

"Cinnamon, deer antler, Cistanche... tiger penis?" Abbe listed the ingredients with a puzzled expression, "You take this for a cold?"

Adam, wearing a pained expression, admitted, "Chief Master, I was wrong. This medicine isn't for me."

The evidence was undeniable, and Adam dared not conceal the truth any longer. He confessed everything about the incident where his two subordinates drugged and tortured Timothy, though he tactfully omitted his own involvement.

"What a bunch of useless fools!" Abbe pinched the bridge of his nose, exasperated beyond measure. "So what did that Shaw fellow say?"

Adam shook his head.

"Nothing at all!?" Abbe nearly laughed out of frustration. "What were you even doing?"

"Chief Master, I think we might have caught the wrong person," Adam said cautiously.

"Oh?" Abbe's eyebrow arched, "Explain."

"I questioned Shaw in detail. He didn't even know who Penelope was, let alone the grudge between Penelope and our Sabra Village. He even made a straw figure, wrote 'Morris' on it, and spends his days pricking it."

"That's interesting." Abbe stroked his chin, pondering for a moment before a smile played on his lips. "I'll go see him."

Abbe carried a bowl of hot medicine to the cell where Timothy was held. From a distance, he could hear sounds of laughter.

"Brother, try this chicken leg."

"Brother, have another drink."

Abbe frowned and approached. Inside, he saw Timothy surrounded by the two subordinates, feasting and drinking merrily.

It turned out that after Timothy had sex with Adam to relieve the effects of the aphrodisiac, Adam, furious, wanted to punish the two subordinates severely. But Timothy intervened, arguing that while they had intended harm, they hadn't actually succeeded. Moreover, killing them would raise questions from Abbe, which wouldn't end well for anyone.

Adam agreed, and after giving each subordinate fifty lashes, the matter was dropped. Since then, the two subordinates treated Timothy like a revered guest, bringing him food and drink.

Timothy sat like a king among them, devouring a chicken leg and gulping down wine.

"Enjoying yourselves, I see," Abbe leaned against the door, watching the scene unfold, "Looks like we're here to serve you, is that it?"

"Ch-Chief Master!" The two subordinates jumped up in fear and quickly backed away from Timothy.

Timothy, still holding the chicken leg, grinned impudently, "Don't want to serve me? Easy. Just let me go."

"Let you go?" Abbe sneered, and in an instant, a cold gleam flashed as he drew his sword, pointing it straight at Timothy.

But Timothy didn't flinch. He sat there, unmoved, even as the sword's edge pressed against his throat, so close it could cut at any moment.

Timothy's mouth opened slightly, and the chicken leg fell into his bowl. He looked up calmly at Abbe.

"I don't even know who you are, so why should I let you go?" Abbe said, his eyes locked on Timothy's.

Timothy replied nonchalantly, "I'm just a commoner. Besides, your subordinates almost killed me. If I were hiding something, I'd have confessed it all then. Why wait till now?"

"The incident with the aphrodisiac was due to my lack of supervision. I apologize on their behalf."

With a thud, Abbe placed a bowl of steaming hot medicine in front of Timothy.

"Adam made this himself. It's great for strengthening the kidneys."

"Thank you, Chief Master." Timothy smiled, taking the bowl and drinking it in one gulp, "Adam already dealt with those two, and they won't dare act out again."

"You're not afraid I poisoned the medicine?" Abbe asked, intrigued.

"I can tell you're a straightforward man, Chief Master. You wouldn't use such underhanded methods," Timothy said, wiping his mouth.

Abbe was moved by his words and scrutinized the man before him—handsome and seemingly rogueish.

Throughout their verbal sparring, Timothy had remained calm and collected. Abbe couldn't find any flaws in his story. If this man was hiding something, his ability to stay composed under threat was impressive.

Abbe had a feeling about Timothy—he wasn't like anyone he'd met before. He began to understand why Adam had spoken up for him. Despite being a prisoner, Timothy had a way of winning people over.

"Stand up," Abbe ordered.

Timothy complied.

In a flash, Abbe's sword sliced through the shackles on Timothy's wrists and ankles, freeing him.

Abbe sheathed his sword and turned his back to Timothy, "I said you had three days to prove your innocence. They're up. You're free to go."

Leaving Timothy standing there, Abbe walked away.

"What!? Chief Master, you let that Shaw guy go!?" The man dressed as a scholar was Lucas Ward, Sabra Village's Second Master. Upon hearing that Abbe had released Timothy, he approached, "Did you confirm his identity?"

"No," Abbe admitted, "but I couldn't prove he was our enemy either. So I had no reason to keep him."

Seeing Abbe's resolve, Lucas had nothing more to say, muttering under his breath, "I hope he's not a spy."

Though Lucas thought Abbe hadn't heard, Abbe had caught every word. He chose not to respond, understanding that Sabra Village was a chaotic place. Lucas, with his suspicious nature, was just being cautious.

Abbe shook his head, brushing off the doubt. He had more pressing matters to attend to than Timothy.

A severe drought had hit Sunder at the start of the year, leaving the village with almost no harvest. Abbe had been leading raids to gather food, adhering to their principle of robbing the rich and sparing the poor. The fierce fighters of Sabra Village, with their deep-seated hatred for the oppressive landlords, were unmatched by government troops, making the local gentry both fearful and helpless against them.

On this particular day, Abbe led over a hundred light cavalry soldiers into fierce combat against the thousand-strong local garrison near Lihu County, northwest of Sabra Village. The local gentry, upon seeing the banner of Sabra Village from afar, were so terrified that they fled without a second thought. Abbe, charging ahead of his men, led the cavalry in a relentless assault on the government troops. In less than fifteen minutes, the troops, numbering ten times more than Nuri's forces, were utterly defeated, abandoning their weapons and fleeing in disarray.

Abbe and his men stormed into the manor, opened the granary, and distributed half of the grain to the impoverished tenant farmers living there. These farmers, who barely had enough to eat, were overjoyed at receiving such a substantial portion of the grain. Many had already heard of Sabra Village's reputation and wanted to follow Abbe, but he politely declined their offers.

After distributing the grain, Abbe and his men returned to their base. Despite their victory and triumphant return, Abbe couldn't find it in himself to be truly happy. He knew that the spoils from this battle would only feed the entire village for a month. And in the Rickie area, they had nearly exhausted all available resources. What would they do for food in a month's time?

With these worries weighing on his mind, Abbe climbed a small hill near their camp. Standing at the summit, he looked out over the desolate landscape of Sunder, ravaged by natural disasters and reduced to barren, cracked earth. Amidst this bleak scenery, the sound of music and celebration could be faintly heard from the pavilions and towers of Rickie, as if it were a world apart from the devastation outside.

"If worse comes to worst, we'll have to attack Rickie," Abbe muttered to himself as he gazed at the prosperous area.

However, Rickie was well-fortified and difficult to assault. Furthermore, Rickie was guarded by Penelope, a formidable opponent. Lost in these chaotic thoughts, Abbe didn't notice the silent approach of footsteps behind him.

Suddenly, a cold wind brushed against his back, jolting Abbe to alertness. He instinctively dodged to the side, a sharp blade slicing past his cheek. Startled, he saw a shadow dart in front of him, but before he could identify the assailant, several more flashes of steel came straight at his face.

"Stop!!" a voice shouted. It was Timothy.

Quick as a flash, Timothy leaped from the shadows, tackling the figure attacking Abbe. The assailant retaliated with a swift sword strike. With a sharp gasp, Timothy fell, paralyzed by the blow.

"Timothy!?" Abbe cried out in shock, rushing forward to kick the sword out of the attacker's hand.

The attacker, clad in black, had his mask torn off by Timothy, revealing his identity—

"Harley!?"

In a flash, Abbe realized that Harley was the weapon sent by Penelope.

"Abbe, prepare to die!" Harley snarled, drawing a dagger from his cloak and lunging at Abbe. But Harley had missed his best chance to kill Abbe. Now prepared, Abbe defended himself staunchly. Despite Harley's fierce attacks, he couldn't get close to Abbe.

Meanwhile, Timothy, enduring excruciating pain from his abdominal wound, crawled slowly on the ground until he grasped a sword lying nearby with his bloodied hand.

Locked in a fierce struggle, Abbe and Harley exchanged several rounds of blows. Harley gradually lost the upper hand. Desperate, he pulled a bag of lime powder from his cloak and flung it into Abbe's face. Caught off guard, Abbe was temporarily blinded, and Harley seized the opportunity to grab his neck and slam him to the ground.

Harley raised his dagger high, ready to deliver the fatal blow.

Suddenly, the sound of a blade piercing flesh rang out. Abbe, expecting the worst, felt no further movement. Slowly, he opened his eyes to see Harley impaled through the chest, his raised arm frozen mid-air, lifeless.

Abbe, heart pounding, looked ahead and saw Timothy's pale, blood-drained face as Harley's body slumped to the ground.

"Ugh..." Timothy coughed up blood, collapsing backward.

"Timothy!!" Abbe cried, rushing to catch him, holding his body, "What happened, Timothy!?"

Timothy clutched his abdomen, blood gushing from the wound, staining his clothes a deep red.

"Am I...going to die?" Timothy asked, looking up at Abbe with a sorrowful smile.

"Don't say that!" Abbe replied shakily, tearing off his sleeve to bandage Timothy's wound. "I'll take you back to the village right now, hang on!"

Timothy truly thought he was going to die this time.

Though Abbe managed to get Timothy back to Sabra Village, he had lost so much blood along the way that he passed out. Abbe, seeing his ashen face, feared the worst and was momentarily paralyzed by panic. Fortunately, Timothy received timely treatment, and by midnight, the bleeding had finally stopped.

After confirming that Timothy was out of danger, Abbe breathed a sigh of relief. He still didn't dare leave Timothy's side, remaining by his bed.

News of Timothy's severe injury while saving Abbe quickly spread throughout Sabra Village, with many coming to visit him late into the night, including Adam. Already exhausted, Abbe had no energy to deal with the crowd at his door. He informed them that Timothy's life was no longer in danger and, citing the need for Timothy to rest, dispersed the onlookers.

That night, Abbe stayed by Timothy's bed, sleepless.

The next day, Timothy finally regained consciousness. When Abbe entered with a bowl of medicinal broth, Timothy was trying to sit up but lacked the strength.

Seeing this, Abbe hurriedly supported him.

"Didn't I tell you to leave yesterday? Why did you come back?" Abbe's tone was reproachful, but his face couldn't hide his deep concern.

Timothy, with Abbe's help, slowly drank the broth.

"I'm alone; I had nowhere else to go." After finishing the medicine, Abbe helped Timothy lean back against the bed. Still pale from blood loss, Timothy gave a weak laugh. "Chief Master probably doesn't know, but yesterday, I was following you the whole time."

Abbe was taken aback: "You mean, when we went to Lihu to seize grain, you were there too?"

Timothy nodded: "I was curious about what kind of place Sabra Village is."

All the way from Poiema to Sunder, Timothy had been pondering how to find a reliable, recruitable force.

In Sunder's current state, the corrupt government left the people destitute, and uprisings were flaring up everywhere, overwhelming the authorities. Despite fighting for so long, the government troops still couldn't defeat Sabra Village. If it wasn't because the government troops were too weak, it meant that Abbe and his men had some unique strengths.

Yesterday's battle confirmed Timothy's suspicions.

Abbe was a capable and strategic leader, and his men, ordinary people struggling to survive in chaotic times, often displayed astonishing combat prowess out of desperation.

This was why the government troops had never been able to overcome Sabra Village.

Having come to Sabra Village by chance, Timothy saw it as fate. If he could use this opportunity to recruit Sabra Village, he might be able to collaborate with Christopher in the court to eliminate Queen's faction.

"Utter nonsense!"

Yet, after hearing Timothy's words, an inexplicable surge of anger flared up in Abbe's heart. Ignoring the fact that Timothy was still a patient, he jabbed his finger into Timothy's chest and shouted, "This is war, not a game! In such chaos, no one knows you. What if someone stabs you to death in the confusion?"

"But if I don't follow you and experience real combat firsthand, I'll never understand the true situation."

"You don't have to risk your life for that." Abbe stared at him, utterly perplexed. "And also on that hill, we are strangers who just met by chance. Why would you take such a big risk to save me?"

"Why?" Timothy hesitated, then gave a bitter smile. "I can't explain it. By the time I realized, my body had already rushed forward."

Abbe was stunned. He gazed at Timothy for a long time, unsure of what to say.

Timothy thought for a moment: "Perhaps it's because, at that moment, I remembered your smile when you distributed the grain to the tenant farmers in Lihu..."

"My smile?" Abbe was puzzled.

"I'm not eloquent enough to describe it..." Timothy looked into Abbe's eyes. "I just felt that your smile was very pleasant, warm, like the sun in spring..."

Caught off guard by Timothy's directness, Abbe felt his ears burn with embarrassment.

"Stop talking nonsense! I'm serious here!"

Trying to hide his inner turmoil, Abbe turned his face away, feigning anger.

"I am serious." Timothy looked earnestly at Abbe. "For that smile, it's worth taking another stab."

Abbe was completely speechless, not knowing how to respond.

Timothy fell silent too. Neither spoke, and an unusual atmosphere quietly spread through the air. Abbe lowered his head for a moment, then glanced up, only to meet Timothy's gaze. The moment their eyes met, Abbe felt as if struck by lightning. He quickly looked away, awkwardly not knowing where to place his hands and feet, and suddenly stood up.

"I... I'll get you another bowl of medicine!" Abbe hastily found an excuse and turned to leave.

"Chief Master!" Timothy called out to him from behind, "I've made up my mind."

Abbe paused, stopping in his tracks.

"I'm not leaving." Timothy, clutching his wound, looked at Abbe and said word by word, "I want to stay in Sabra Village."

Timothy seemed to be seeking Abbe's approval. He waited silently for a long time, and finally, Abbe softly uttered, "Do as you please," then rushed out, his figure disappearing from Timothy's sight.

Chapter Seventeen: Where Affection Begins

Timothy smoothly became part of Sabra Village and boldly moved into Abbe's house, beginning their cohabitation.

In fact, Timothy didn't intentionally take advantage of Abbe. It was Abbe who suggested this arrangement to conveniently care for Timothy. It seemed that the fact Timothy had taken a stab for him had deeply impacted Abbe, making him feel the need to compensate for it.

For example, when it came to taking care of Timothy, Abbe liked to do things himself. Since Timothy's internal organs were injured by the stab and he couldn't eat solid food, Abbe personally cooked congee and made soup for him.

"Is it good?" Abbe anxiously watched Timothy as he slowly drank the congee he made.

"Good... it's good." Timothy looked up, forcing a smile.

However, Timothy had to admit that Abbe's cooking skills were horrendous. He never knew congee could be made so unappetizing. But being taken care of, he couldn't complain and had gotten used to forcing down the so-called congee.

"That's good!" Abbe sighed in relief, wiping the sweat from his forehead, revealing his scarred fingers. "I never cooked before, so I was worried you might not like my food."

I can see that, Timothy thought, but maintained a calm expression, "Actually, I'm easy to please. I can eat anything, no problem."

"Indeed, you're even easier to feed than a dog." Abbe patted Timothy's shoulder, grinning. "Sometimes when I feed our dog, it barks in protest. Its taste is more picky than yours."

"Hey! Are you saying I'm worse than a dog?" Timothy protested, pretending to be upset.

Hearing this, Timothy found it amusing, and Abbe laughed heartily too. They exchanged a glance and couldn't help but burst into laughter.

Though Abbe's food was hard to eat, considering his effort to cook for him, Timothy couldn't bear to criticize him.

Thinking this, the congee in the bowl seemed a bit more palatable.

"Don't rush, or you'll choke," Abbe chuckled, "Eat slowly, and after you finish, I'll take you somewhere."

Since accepting Timothy, Abbe enjoyed taking him around whenever they had free time. Thanks to this, in just a week, Timothy had familiarized himself with every nook and cranny of Sabra Village and its surroundings.

Today, Abbe brought Timothy to the training ground.

"Chief Master, why did you bring me here?" Timothy asked, puzzled.

"Although I agreed to let you join Sabra Village, we don't support idlers here. Without skills, you won't earn the respect of our brothers." Abbe walked to the weapon rack, his eyes scanning the array of weapons. "I noticed during your fight with that guy named Chai, you were agile but lacked proper training. It's a pity."

Timothy was taken aback: "Chief Master, are you going to teach me martial arts?"

"No rush." Abbe smiled and shook his head. "You're still recovering. Besides, martial arts aren't the most important thing in warfare."

"Martial arts aren't important? What is?" Timothy asked curiously.

"Archery and horsemanship." Abbe picked up a bow and arrows, nocked an arrow, and aimed at a target a hundred paces away.

Abbe was wearing a white and blue fitted robe, his extended arms smooth and long, his waist straight and strong like a pine tree on a snowy mountain. As he focused on the target, he resembled a statue, inspiring awe and making it hard to look away.

Timothy watched Abbe in fascination, forgetting to breathe.

With a sudden whoosh, Abbe's arrow flew like a shooting star, hitting the bullseye a hundred paces away.

Timothy was so amazed he forgot to clap or cheer.

Abbe turned around, seriously saying, "Show me your arm."

Timothy snapped out of his daze and lifted his sleeve, revealing his muscular arm.

"As I thought." Abbe placed a hand on Timothy's biceps, admiringly. "When I saw you tackle Harley and tear off his mask, I knew you had great strength. I wasn't wrong. Timothy, you're a natural for archery and horsemanship."

Pleased with the compliment, Timothy's spirits soared: "Chief Master, I want to learn archery and horsemanship from you! Teach me!"

Abbe winked: "I'm a strict teacher, you know?"

Timothy's eyes sparkled: "I wouldn't have it any other way!"

"Alright, give it a try."

Abbe handed the bow and arrows to Timothy, guiding his stance.

"Steady your stance, spread your legs wider."

"Yes, Chief Master!"

Abbe stood close behind Timothy, adjusting his posture with a firm grip on his waist and a light kick to his leg: "Why are you shaking? Are you having a fit?"

Timothy felt a rush of heat. Abbe was too close, his breath on Timothy's face making it hard to concentrate.

"Archery requires unity of mind and arrow. If your heart wavers, so will your arrow." Abbe gently lifted Timothy's hand, "Stay calm and focus."

Timothy steadied his mind and aimed.

With a swoosh, the arrow flew, hitting the edge of the target.

Seeing Timothy's disappointment, Abbe patted his shoulder: "It's normal for a first try. Not missing the target completely is good."

"Was my form correct?" Timothy asked, looking at Abbe.

"You were too tense when releasing. Remember, the release should be as gentle as possible; otherwise, the bow's vibration will affect your accuracy."

Demonstrating again, Abbe smoothly nocked, drew, and released three arrows, all hitting the bullseye.

"See? My bow doesn't move when I shoot."

"I understand now. Let me try again!" Timothy regained his enthusiasm and nocked another arrow.

That day, Timothy shot over a hundred arrows on the training ground. By sunset, the targets were almost fully pierced. Reluctantly, Timothy stopped and put down the bow.

On the way back to the village, Timothy's excitement didn't fade as he eagerly discussed his day's practice with Abbe. Abbe listened with a smile, occasionally nodding and offering advice.

"You really enjoyed it, didn't you?" Abbe smiled at Timothy.

"You're a great teacher!" Timothy wiped the sweat from his forehead, beaming.

"By the way, when we're alone it's fine, but don't call me Chief Master in front of the others," Abbe suddenly remembered and said.

"Why not?" Timothy asked, puzzled.

"Taking on a student is just for fun. I never take apprentices se-riously. If the others see me making an exception for you, they might be unhappy."

For fun? For some reason, Timothy felt a pang of emptiness at these words.

"Huh? Your hand—" Abbe suddenly exclaimed, grabbing Timo-thy's hand.

"What?" Timothy looked at his hand, noticing a blood blister on his thumb from practicing too hard.

"You're bleeding!" Abbe frowned, his eyes showing concern. "Why didn't you say anything?"

"I didn't notice..." Timothy scratched his head, smiling sheepish-ly.

Before he could react, Abbe held Timothy's hand and gently sucked on the wound, his lips brushing against it lightly, drawing out the blood.

Timothy stared at Abbe in a daze, his mind blank.

Unaware of Timothy's reaction, Abbe finished tending to the wound and looked up, their eyes meeting. Abbe hesitated, then quickly released Timothy's hand, looking slightly embarrassed.

A surge of warmth filled Timothy's heart, beating wildly like lava about to erupt.

Abbe casually turned away, brushing a strand of hair from his face. Timothy couldn't help but notice a faint blush on Abbe's ear.

Just like when Timothy lay in bed talking to Abbe, the air grew quiet. To ease the awkwardness, Abbe walked ahead quickly. Af-ter a few steps, he noticed Timothy hadn't followed and turned back, seeing him standing there.

"Why are you standing there? Hurry up and catch up!"

Abbe stood in the glow of the setting sun, the blush on his cheeks resembling the evening clouds of spring, unconsciously painting Timothy's heart with a tender hue.

Having narrowly escaped death, Timothy seemed to have a new lease on life. Not only did he recover quickly, but his physical condition also improved significantly. After half a month, his wounds were nearly healed, and he gradually returned to a normal diet.

Despite his recovery, Abbe insisted on taking care of Timothy's meals. Abbe, who seemed to have developed a sudden interest in cooking, was eager to prepare food for Timothy. Whether Abbe's culinary skills had improved or Timothy's palate had adjusted, Timothy found Abbe's food less unpalatable than before. But Abbe's changes didn't stop there. Lately, Timothy noticed that Abbe often wore a worried expression and sighed deeply while staring into the distance when he was alone. Timothy was curious but didn't know how to ask. It wasn't until Abbe gathered his men in the Hall of Heroes to discuss important matters that Timothy learned what was troubling Abbe.

"The reason I've gathered you all today is that our grain supplies are running low. At best, we can last until the end of the month. We need to find a way to gather more grain. What are your suggestions?" Abbe began directly, wasting no time.

"We've already raided all the nearby places," Adam said, frowning. "Should we try raiding the same places again and hope for better luck?"

"Places we've already raided will have even less grain and will be more heavily guarded. It's not worth it," Abbe shook his head, rejecting Adam's suggestion.

"I think we should consider relocating Sabra Village to find food elsewhere. What do you think, Chief Master?" Lucas, the Second Master, proposed, causing an uproar in the Hall of Heroes as everyone began discussing it fervently.

"This..." Abbe looked troubled, "While it's not impossible..."

"Sabra Village is our hard-earned home. How can we abandon it so easily?" A voice in the crowd quickly objected.

"Yes, we all have families. In these dangerous times, we might die on the way before finding a new place to settle."

"But if we stay here, we'll starve. We might as well take a gamble and relocate," someone else supported Lucas, and the hall quickly turned into a heated debate.

However, Abbe didn't agree with either side. For him, the only solution for Sabra Village was to take Rickie. But this plan was extremely risky, and even he couldn't make up his mind just yet.

He scanned the hall, noticing that amidst the noisy crowd, one person remained silent and thoughtful.

"Timothy, what do you think?" Abbe asked, turning to Timothy.

"Me?" Timothy seemed surprised that Abbe would seek his opinion. He hesitated, "Is it appropriate for me to speak? I've only been here for half a month..."

"There's nothing inappropriate about it," Abbe replied straightforwardly. "Since you've joined Sabra Village, you're one of us. Don't consider yourself an outsider. I want to hear your thoughts."

"In that case, I'll speak frankly," Timothy said, as if making up his mind. "I think we should dig a secret tunnel."

"A secret tunnel?" Abbe was taken aback.

"Were you daydreaming, Shaw?" Lucas sneered. "We're discussing our grain shortage, not digging tunnels."

"I know exactly what we're discussing," Timothy responded calmly, "Sabra Village is already small, and now we face a grain shortage. If I were the commander of Rickie, I'd take this opportunity to surround Sabra Village. Without a single soldier, we'd be defeated within half a month due to lack of supplies."

Timothy's words brought silence to the Hall of Heroes.

"You mean we should prepare a retreat?" Abbe asked thoughtfully.

"Whether it's a retreat or not, it's uncertain. But with a secret tunnel, we can avoid the enemy's surveillance and launch surprise attacks. Our ultimate goal shouldn't be to hold Sabra Village but to take Rickie."

Abbe felt a surge of joy. Timothy's thinking coincided with his own plans.

Timothy continued, "Since a battle with Rickie is inevitable, we should prepare in advance, or we'll face disaster soon."

"Nonsense!" Lucas retorted dismissively. "The urgent problem is our current grain shortage. Digging a tunnel requires manpower, which means more grain consumption. Your idea not only fails to solve the problem but makes it worse!"

"Finding grain is possible," Timothy said confidently.

"Then go find some!" Lucas challenged.

Seeing the two arguing, Abbe quickly intervened.

"Uncle," Abbe walked over and patted Lucas's shoulder. "You're right. We need to address the grain shortage immediately."

Lucas, feeling supported by Abbe, smirked at Timothy.

"But," Abbe continued, turning to Timothy, "Timothy also has a point. We must plan for the future as well as address the present crisis. In my view, gathering grain and digging a tunnel are not mutually exclusive."

"Chief Master!" Lucas exclaimed, "But digging a tunnel requires more grain. How will we solve that?"

Abbe nodded, thinking for a moment before addressing both men. "Here's what we'll do. Uncle, you'll oversee the tunnel construction. As for the urgent matter of grain, Timothy will handle it. How does that sound?"

Timothy confidently pounded his chest. "Leave it to me!"

Abbe turned to Lucas with a smile. "Uncle, any objections now?"

Lucas had no choice but to grunt in reluctant agreement.

Chapter Eighteen: Gains and Losses

"So, you came to Rickie just to ask me to lend grain to a group of bandits!?"

On the Rickie River, a fishing boat drifted along. Inside the boat, Timothy, dressed as a boatman in a straw raincoat and a bamboo hat, sat across from the King of Nixie, who wore simple, modest blue cloth clothes. They spoke in hushed tones.

"Your Highness, King of Nixie, I'm in a dire situation," Timothy said, pouring a drink for the King of Nixie from a small jug. "Besides, this is only a loan. Once it's done, I'll repay you with interest."

"Once it's done..." The King of Nixie sipped his drink, smiling enigmatically at Timothy. "It's not that I can't lend the grain, but I'm really curious, Timothy. What exactly are you planning with this group?"

Timothy's heart skipped a beat as he met the King of Nixie's eyes, which were identical to Christopher's. The sharp gaze seemed to probe Timothy's inner thoughts. Unsure whether to reveal his plan, Timothy pondered for a moment and decided to take a gamble.

"If I'm honest, will Your Highness lend me the grain?"

"That depends on what you have to say."

"What if I told you that everything I'm doing is to save the Emperor?"

The King of Nixie was stunned, eyes widening as he looked at Timothy.

"I plan to recruit this group to coordinate with the palace and eliminate Queen Owen!" Timothy whispered. "Your Highness must be loyal to the Emperor. Otherwise, you wouldn't have rebuked Bowie for oppressing the Crown Prince, right?"

The King of Nixie smiled bitterly. "You've seen through my intentions."

He sighed deeply, looking at Timothy with a serious expression. "Alright, I can lend you the grain, but not too much, or Penelope will get suspicious."

At the mention of Penelope, Timothy couldn't help but feel a surge of resentment.

"Your Highness, please don't tell Morris about my plan. He's wronged me so badly, and I'm looking for a chance to get back at him."

"It seems you had a rough time with him."

The King of Nixie had already heard the details of how Timothy ended up in Sabra Village. Hearing Timothy's words now, he chuckled meaningfully.

"Mr. Shaw, there's something I should tell you."

"Please go ahead, Your Highness."

"I've heard a bit about Sabra Village from Penelope. Indeed, this group of guerilla fighters is formidable, especially their leader Abbe, who excels in archery and swordsmanship. But when it comes to strategy, Penelope is superior."

"That's..."

Seeing Timothy speechless, the King of Nixie continued, "Moreover, the Morris family has always been loyal to the throne. If Penelope knew you were recruiting troops to support the Emperor, she would likely help."

"What!?" Timothy slammed the table. "Your Highness, are you suggesting I collaborate with Penelope!?"

"Mr. Shaw, calm down." The King of Nixie patted Timothy's shoulder. "To achieve great things, one must look at the bigger picture. If you truly care about the Emperor, you should prioritize the greater good over personal grudges. Don't you agree?"

"That makes sense, but I can't swallow my anger!" Timothy fumed, pounding the table. "Besides, everyone in Sabra Village wants to get rid of Penelope. How can we work with her? Are you serious, Your Highness?"

"I was just suggesting it. You can take it as a passing remark," the King of Nixie waved nonchalantly. "But you're right, Penelope has always looked down on the bandits of Sabra Village. Getting her to cooperate would be difficult. However, consider my proposal. There's strength in numbers, isn't there?"

Timothy remained silent for a while before shrugging. "Fine, we'll deal with Penelope later. Even if we have to work with her, let me settle my grudge first."

"You..." The King of Nixie sighed with a bitter smile, then suddenly remembered something and pulled out a letter. "I almost forgot. This is for you."

"A letter?" Timothy took the letter, seeing his name written in elegant handwriting.

Is it from the Emperor?

Heart racing, Timothy opened the letter and read it carefully. The contents were mundane, filled with trivial matters from the palace, yet it conveyed Christopher's loneliness and longing. Timothy felt a pang of emotion, wanting to write back but having no pen and paper.

"You want to reply?" The King of Nixie, reading Timothy's expression, pulled out a writing set from his bundle.

"Your Highness!?" Timothy was astonished. "You're too prepared!"

The King of Nixie smiled as he ground ink. "I figured you'd want to reply after reading the letter."

Timothy picked up the brush, writing a brief response. Unlike Christopher, who could write at length about trivial matters, Timothy simply assured the Emperor that he was well and making progress, promising to return soon. He carefully folded the letter and handed it to the King of Nixie.

As they prepared to part, Timothy voiced a question that had been on his mind.

"Your Highness, there's something I've been wondering."

"Ask away. We're in this together now," the King of Nixie replied.

"What's your relationship with the Emperor? Why do you look so much alike?"

The King of Nixie fell silent for a long time before sighing. "Do you know the identity of the late Dowager Empress?"

Timothy shook his head.

The King of Nixie's eyes darkened as he looked down. "Amanda Cook...was once my most beloved concubine. When the late Emperor visited my residence, he took a liking to her and brought her into the palace as his consort. Soon after, she was found to be pregnant."

Timothy was shocked. "Are you saying...the Dowager Empress was carrying your..."

The King of Nixie placed a finger on Timothy's lips, shaking his head. "Don't say it. It doesn't matter anymore. What matters is that he is the rightful ruler of Great Alvah, the true sovereign."

Timothy looked at the King of Nixie with mixed feelings, understanding the unusual bond between him and Christopher. This revelation strengthened Timothy's belief that he had chosen the right side. With the King of Nixie's support, rescuing Christopher from peril was no longer a distant dream.

The King of Nixie, generous as always, lent Timothy enough grain to sustain Sabra Village for a month.

However, when Timothy returned to Sabra Village with the good news, he was met with unexpected hostility.

"You want us to rely on the King of Nixie!?"

The mention of the King of Nixie turned Abbe's face dark with rage.

Confused, Timothy hadn't revealed that he borrowed grain from the King of Nixie. Instead, he cautiously asked Abbe at the next Hall of Heroes meeting whether they should consider co-operating with the King of Nixie.

But Timothy's question seemed to hit a nerve. Not only Abbe, but everyone else fell silent, exchanging uneasy glances.

"Why? What's the problem?" Timothy asked carefully.

"The problem?" Abbe stood up abruptly, glaring at Timothy. "We at Sabra Village are sworn enemies of the court! You think I, Abbe, will bow to them for a mere pittance? Never!"

"Chief Master, that's not what I meant! I'm talking about coop-eration, not submission to the court!" Timothy tried to explain.

"What's the difference!?" Abbe shook off Timothy's hand. "To them, we're just disposable pawns, to be used and discarded!"

Before Timothy could respond, Lucas spoke up.

"Well, well, isn't it interesting how our Mr. Shaw quickly found a noble backer," Lucas sneered, his words dripping with sarcasm.

Chapter Eighteen: Gains and Losses

"Chief Master, now you should see, this Shaw is just an outsider. He doesn't understand you, nor does he understand Sabra Village's situation. I've said all along he's unreliable, always siding with outsiders. See, I was right, wasn't I?"

"Timothy is not that kind of person!" Adam finally couldn't stand it anymore and stood up, "Timothy is also thinking about what's best for the village. He just doesn't understand the situation. It's unfair to say that about him!"

"Adam..." Timothy was taken aback. He didn't expect Adam to stand up for him at this moment.

"Your naivety is a virtue, but there are more bad people than good in this world. You need to be more cautious when dealing with others, or you'll end up taking a hard fall. Don't say your uncle didn't warn you."

"Enough!"

Abbe, unable to tolerate it any longer, cut him off sharply. He looked up and met Timothy's eyes, and Timothy's heart trembled.

Abbe's eyes were red, and his gaze seemed to blaze with an unspeakable mixture of anger and frustration.

"Timothy, you've disappointed me deeply." Abbe said each word with weight, "I never thought you'd be someone who panders to power!"

With that, Abbe gave Timothy no chance to explain and stormed out, disappearing from everyone's sight.

As Abbe left, murmurs spread through the crowd. Adam sighed deeply, muttering to himself, "I never thought I'd see the Chief Master so angry."

Meanwhile, Lucas walked by Timothy with a smug expression, whispering, "So, this is all you're capable of."

Timothy clenched his fists silently, his face set with determination.

After the tumultuous meeting in the Hall of Heroes, Abbe saddled a horse and rode out of the village. Wanting to be alone, he forbade anyone from following. Timothy didn't know where he went until Abbe returned at sunset, riding back slowly.

Timothy intended to talk to Abbe once he returned, but that evening, Abbe didn't come back to their shared house. Growing anxious, Timothy went out to look for him. He learned from others that Abbe had gone to Lucas's house and hadn't left.

Timothy found Lucas's residence and saw a light still on inside, with voices coming from within. He quietly approached the door and heard Lucas's voice.

"I don't understand. What's so special about Timothy? Why is the Chief Master so concerned about an outsider?"

Hearing this, Timothy stopped, curious about Abbe's true thoughts. Abbe had treated him well, but Lucas's jealousy indicated that Abbe's feelings might be unique.

Abbe's reply was slow in coming, then he sighed deeply and said, "He saved my life, after all."

"So what if he saved your life?" Lucas retorted, "I saved you too. Have you forgotten how we escaped death together?"

"Of course not, Uncle. I'll never forget your kindness."

Timothy was stunned. He hadn't known the exact nature of the relationship between Lucas and Abbe, but it seemed they had a bond forged through life and death experiences.

Lucas's tone softened, "Abbe, don't blame your uncle for meddling. Mr. Simpson's dying words still echo in my ears. I swore to protect you with my life."

"Uncle..." Abbe's voice wavered with emotion.

"Ever since Sabra Village defeated the Sunder soldiers, more people have come to join us. With a bigger group, we have more problems. I worry we'll be destroyed from within rather than by our enemies. I can't sleep at night because of this."

"It's my fault as Chief Master for making you worry," Abbe said softly.

"No, you've done well. You've united the people and led us in battle. Let me handle the other matters. I just can't trust this Shaw. He's been here for a while but says nothing about himself. We still don't know who he really is. How can we trust him?"

"But..." Abbe chose his words carefully, "Everyone has secrets. If he doesn't want to share, we shouldn't pry."

"Chief Master, you weren't so lenient with the spy we captured," Lucas argued. "Everyone sees how you favor Shaw, who's done nothing to earn it. What do you expect the others to think?"

Abbe persisted, "But he's just arrived. We need to give him a chance to prove himself."

Lucas scoffed, "I fear he'll bring trouble before he has a chance to prove anything."

"Don't say such unlucky things. Uncle, you've been stressed with so many worries lately. You should rest more and think less."

"Chief Master..."

Lucas seemed about to say more, but Abbe cut him off, changing the subject, "It's late. Let's rest."

With a sudden blow, the candle was extinguished.

"Uncle, remember when Father was still alive, we often talked by candlelight, and you told me stories of knights and heroes. It's been years since I heard one of your stories."

Lucas chuckled, "You were just a child then. Aren't you too old for bedtime stories now?"

Abbe laughed, "Of course not! You know how I love tales of knights and adventure. I can never get enough!"

Lucas sighed, "Alright, alright. Let me think. What story should I tell tonight...?"

Timothy didn't hear what they said next. Knowing Abbe wouldn't return that night, he turned away and left quietly.

Chapter Nineteen: Proximity to Virtue

In the end, Timothy still didn't understand why Abbe was so kind to him. He only knew that if he continued to rely on Abbe's goodwill without making an effort, it would inevitably lead to endless trouble.

After all, Sabra Village didn't belong to Abbe alone. Winning over Abbe wasn't enough; Timothy needed the support of the entire village. To do this, he had to prove his sincerity with his abilities, earning the respect of the brothers in Sabra Village and dispelling Lucas's doubts.

Otherwise, his recruitment plan might fail before it even started. If only there was someone else in Sabra Village besides Abbe who had significant influence.

Thinking this, a name quickly surfaced in his mind—Adam.

Today in the Hall of Heroes, when Lucas openly questioned Timothy, Adam was the only one who stood up for him. Adam seemed to be one of Abbe's trusted confidants, but unlike the suspicious Lucas, Adam was straightforward and kind-hearted. As the first person in Sabra Village to interact with Timothy, and given their physical encounter, Timothy felt it necessary to build a good relationship with him.

With this in mind, Timothy went to Adam's house. Seeing the light still on, he knew Adam hadn't gone to bed. Overjoyed, Timothy pushed the door open, not realizing it was only half-closed. He stumbled in, nearly falling into the room.

"Who is it!?" Adam, lying on his bed with his back to the door, seemed to be looking at something. Hearing the door, he quickly hid what he was holding under the covers and looked up in a panic.

"Timothy!?"

Adam was stunned to see Timothy.

"Sorry, I didn't know your door was open. Sabra Village is really peaceful, not even locking doors at night. Impressive! Hahaha!" Timothy babbled, trying to ease the awkwardness.

"What brings you here?" Adam quickly got up and welcomed Timothy in. "Aren't you staying with the Chief Master?"

"Chief Master isn't sleeping in our place tonight. He's with Second Master." Timothy looked around nervously. "Can I sleep here tonight?"

Adam paused, not replying immediately.

Thinking Adam was reluctant, Timothy quickly added, "I'll sleep on the floor, not the bed."

Adam shook his head vigorously. "That won't do! You're a guest. How can I let you sleep on the floor?"

"No, I'm not a guest, and you're not the host." Timothy placed his hand on Adam's slender shoulder and smiled warmly, "We're brothers, right?"

"Brothers..."

"Brothers are about hierarchy, not age. You joined Sabra Village before me, you're skilled, and you're the Chief Master's right-hand man. It's not too much to call you brother, is it?"

Flattered by Timothy's praise, Adam blushed and lowered his head, "Do you have a nickname or something?"

"Call me Alan."

"Alan..." Adam's eyes lit up. "Can I call you Alan then?"

"Of course. Call me whatever you like. By the way, what were you looking at just now? You seemed very secretive."

Timothy climbed onto Adam's bed, trying to lift the covers, but Adam quickly threw himself over them, pressing down hard.

"Nothing! I was almost asleep, you must have seen wrong!"

Adam hugged his legs, sitting firmly on the covers. Timothy smirked at him knowingly, "I see."

Adam, feeling guilty, averted his eyes.

"Why are you blushing?" Timothy leaned closer.

Realizing his face was hot, Adam stammered, "It's the candle-light."

To hide his embarrassment, he turned and blew out the candle, plunging the room into darkness. Not seeing Adam's flushed face, Timothy felt a bit disappointed but didn't push further. He yawned exaggeratedly and lay down beside him.

Seeing Timothy finally let it go, Adam relaxed and lay down as well.

"Adam."

"Yeah?"

In the darkness, only moonlight filtered through the window, casting a soft silver glow on the floor.

Thinking of the day's events, Timothy felt a flood of emotions. The King of Nixie, Christopher, Abbe, Sabra Village, and that detestable Penelope—all these matters entangled his mind like a tangled web, tugging at his heart.

"Alan, are you still thinking about the Chief Master?"

"Yes..." Timothy sighed, "I know so little about him. You must know him well, right, Adam?"

Adam shook his head, "I wouldn't say very well. The Chief Master found me a year ago when I was fleeing for my life. In Sabra Village, the one who knows him best is Uncle Lucas."

Thinking of Lucas, Timothy couldn't help asking, "What exactly is the relationship between the Chief Master and the Second Master? Why are they so close?"

"The Chief Master's family was once very prestigious, and his father, Mr. Simpson, was an official. Uncle Lucas was a retainer in

Mr. Simpson's household and watched the Chief Master grow up. When trouble befell the Simpson family, Uncle Lucas protected the Chief Master from the court's persecution. They're not related by blood, but their bond is like father and son. Since losing his father, the Chief Master treats Uncle Lucas with utmost respect."

Hearing this, Timothy understood. No wonder their conversation outside Lucas's door had that mysterious familiarity. They had such a deep connection.

"Second Master doesn't look that old," Timothy mused. "But he's like a senior in the village."

"I heard he's almost fifty." Adam laughed, "Can't tell, right? He used to be a monk, and he takes great care of his health, so he looks much younger."

"That explains why Abbe respects him so much. It seems Second Master is indeed the most important figure in our village."

"Those who endure hardship together share a deep bond," Adam said.

"More than that. By age, rank, and experience, Uncle could have led Sabra Village himself, but he let the Chief Master take charge. That's quite remarkable."

"Is it? I don't understand why it's special."

"Of course, it's special. The hardest thing in this world isn't sharing hardship but sharing wealth. Some people stand by you in tough times but betray you for a bit of glory and profit. History is full of such examples." Timothy turned to look at Adam, "But you, Adam, are pure-hearted and loyal. No wonder you don't understand such people."

Adam blushed again in the dark.

Timothy's compliments were sincere and subtle, always making others feel warm. Adam was no exception. Wanting to be modest but not knowing how, he sweetly accepted Timothy's praise.

"Isn't Alan the same?" Adam asked softly, gazing at Timothy.

"I'm not that noble. If fame and fortune were in front of me, I might be tempted too," Timothy replied seriously.

"Nonsense! I don't believe it!" Adam grabbed Timothy's hand, "You're not that kind of person."

Timothy chuckled softly and shook Adam's hand firmly. "I'm just a mere mortal with all sorts of desires, but I believe that good company makes one better. From now on, I'll follow you, Adam. Please use your righteousness to cleanse me of my greed and vulgarity."

"I'm not as good as you think," Adam said, lowering his eyes slowly. After a moment of silence, he continued, "Actually, I have worldly desires too... Ever since that day with you... I..."

As he spoke, Adam's voice grew quieter and quieter, until it was almost a whisper. Whether Timothy heard him or not, Adam couldn't tell. He waited silently, his heart tumultuous, but Timothy never responded. After a while, he heard light snoring beside him. Timothy had fallen asleep, still holding his hand.

Timothy had a dream. He dreamt that Poiema Palace was under siege, Christopher was tightly bound by the rebels, dragged to the city gate with a gleaming knife at his throat. Timothy himself, wearing a red-plumed helmet and golden armor, with a jeweled sword at his waist and a carved bow on his back, charged into the enemy ranks alone. He reached the city gate, drew his bow, and shot an arrow right into the rebel leader's forehead. Enraged, the rebel's men pushed Christopher off the city wall, sending him plummeting down.

In a panic, Timothy shouted for the emperor. Suddenly, it was as if wings sprouted from his back. He leaped off his horse and caught Christopher mid-air.

"Timothy, I knew you would come..." Christopher nestled in Timothy's arms, gently running his fingers over Timothy's firm chest, softly pinching his nipples.

"Is the emperor that eager?" Timothy, feeling hot all over from Christopher's touch, grabbed the mischievous hand and whispered, "The ministers and soldiers are watching."

"Then let them watch." Dreaming Christopher was unexpectedly bold. He flipped Timothy onto the ground, straddled him, and, while undressing and gasping, said, "I want you now!"

With that, he leaned down and kissed Timothy passionately. Timothy, his mind clouded by Christopher's kiss, felt his desire rising. He grabbed Christopher's now-exposed buttocks, spread them wide, and thrust his already erect member inside.

"Ah... Ah..."

Christopher moaned shamelessly, gyrating on Timothy with abandon. He didn't care about the dignity of a monarch, flaunting his lewdness for all to see. Timothy, unable to hold back any longer, pounded into Christopher with reckless abandon, satisfying his lust in full view of everyone.

Timothy had had erotic dreams before. In the past, he would always wake up at the crucial moment, but this time, the pleasure was vivid and inexplicably prolonged.

After the climax, Christopher continued to caress and kiss his body, but his face gradually blurred, becoming indistinct.

"Emperor...?" Timothy rubbed his eyes. "Is that you, Emperor?"

Timothy reached out to touch Christopher's face, but he turned into a wisp of smoke and disappeared.

Timothy woke with a start in the darkness, turning his head to see Adam leaning beside him, his hand resting on Timothy's chest. His shirt had slipped off his shoulders, exposing a broad expanse of bare chest.

"Adam? What are you doing?" Timothy asked in surprise.

Adam jolted, as if greatly frightened. He quickly withdrew his hand and retreated to the corner.

"Sorry, I sleep badly," he mumbled, keeping his head down, not daring to meet Timothy's eyes.

This isn't just a matter of bad sleeping habits. How do you explain the shirt?

But Timothy didn't intend to pursue the matter. Ignorance was bliss in such situations. He murmured an acknowledgment, lazily turned his back to Adam, and pretended to go back to sleep.

After that, Adam didn't approach Timothy again. That night, the two slept far apart, one at each end of the bed. Timothy, full of doubts, eventually succumbed to drowsiness and fell back into a deep sleep, saying nothing more.

The next morning when Timothy woke up, Adam was already gone.

Timothy climbed out of bed, dazed. The events of the previous night replayed vividly in his mind.

Adam was too suspicious. He had been sneaky when Timothy entered, and who knew what he had been up to at night. Timothy glanced at the bed beside him; it had been tidied up perfectly.

But Timothy's curiosity was piqued. He searched everywhere: under the pillow, in the bedding, every possible hiding place. Finally, he found a clue under a slightly raised floor tile. Carefully lifting the tile, he discovered a book hidden underneath. Opening it, he realized it was an erotic novel.

Timothy quickly flipped through the book, a knowing smile playing at the corners of his mouth.

Chapter Twenty: A Turn of Events

Abbe and Timothy started a cold war.

For several days in a row, Abbe was either not in the village or avoiding Timothy entirely, not showing up all day. Meanwhile, Lucas continued to mock Timothy whenever he had the chance. Timothy, however, changed his attitude and treated Lucas with utmost respect, calling him "uncle" at every turn. Initially, Lucas got goosebumps hearing Timothy call him that and looked at him as if he were crazy, but Timothy didn't mind, persistently warming up to Lucas, who couldn't find a way to deal with him. While the tunnels of Sabra Village were being dug fervently, the grain from the King of Nixie arrived. Of course, Timothy didn't mention that it was a gift from the King of Nixie. Instead, he secretly transported it back, piling it into the granary without anyone noticing. Since he moved it bit by bit, no one noticed whether the grain had increased or decreased.

However, as the saying goes, "Walking by the river often, how can your shoes not get wet?" Timothy thought he was sneaky enough, but a week later, Adam caught him in the act.

"Alan! Are you crazy??" Adam exclaimed in disbelief after hearing Timothy's explanation. "Do you know if Chief Master finds out, he will unhesitatingly banish you from the village!"

"But I couldn't think of any other way at the moment," Timothy replied helplessly.

"And didn't you say you're a commoner? How come you know the King of Nixie? What's your relationship with him? Why would he lend you grain?" Adam pressed on.

"Didn't I once infiltrate Pavilion Lainey with Penelope?" Timothy's mind raced. "I made up an identity then, claiming to be Penelope's distant cousin, and that's how I got in touch with the King of Nixie."

Adam frowned slightly and looked at Timothy in silence.

"Really, Adam! You have to believe me! I had no intention of harming Sabra Village, or let heaven strike me down if I—"

Before Timothy could finish, Adam hurriedly covered his mouth.

"Alright, alright, I believe you!" Adam whispered. "But Alan, please, let's not do this again, okay? I don't want to see you get banished."

"Adam..." Timothy felt warmth in his chest and gently held Adam's hand. "You're so good to me."

Adam blushed, gently pulling his hand away from Timothy's grasp. "Alan, if you find gathering grain difficult, let me help you."

Timothy's eyes widened. "Do you have a good idea, Adam?"

Adam sighed. "Well, it's not really a good idea, more like a desperate measure. We can scout around the nearby areas and see if we can find any loopholes. Even though the grain we gather this way might be a drop in the bucket, it's better than borrowing from the King of Nixie."

Timothy's heart sank again, but looking into Adam's earnest eyes, he couldn't refuse. After a moment of contemplation, he nodded. "Alright, I'll listen to you, Adam."

In the following days, Timothy and Adam left early and returned late, patrolling and scouting the surroundings. However, after a week, the results were as expectedly dismal. The nearby villages were either nearly deserted or heavily guarded. Moreover, Sabra Village wasn't the only one scavenging for grain; rumors had it that Sunder was overrun with bandits and refugees, causing merchants to avoid the area. The vast, desolate lands were sparsely populated.

But just when Timothy and Adam were about to lose hope, luck unexpectedly smiled upon them. One day, as they patrolled two hundred miles southwest of Nuri, they stumbled upon a grain convoy. The convoy had three carts, each driven by a coachman and escorted by four soldiers. A banner bearing the word "Morris" fluttered atop the carts.

Fortune favors the bold. Hiding in the shadows, Timothy nudged Adam's arm. "Adam, there are twelve of them. Can you handle it?"

Adam gritted his teeth, rolling up his sleeves. "Even if I can't, we have to fight to survive!"

Timothy, equally eager, added, "I can finally test my archery skills."

Adam whispered, "Don't be reckless. Follow my lead. If things go south, retreat immediately. Don't worry about me, just make sure you escape."

Timothy nodded. "Got it, Adam. You be careful too!"

The two quickly devised a plan. Timothy would shoot the horses' legs first, then Adam would charge out to draw fire. Meanwhile, Timothy would shoot the remaining horses from the rear. Throughout the operation, Timothy would stay hidden, providing cover for Adam.

With their plan set, they sprang into action.

Timothy's hard practice paid off. His first arrow hit a horse's leg precisely. At the same time, Adam charged out from the bushes, catching the soldiers off guard and swiftly slitting the throats of two soldiers before they could react.

The convoy fell into chaos. As planned, Timothy quickly shot two more arrows, targeting the rear horses. One arrow hit a horse's abdomen, and the other hit the reins.

Then, something miraculous happened. The last horse, spooked, broke free from its reins and bolted forward, trampling a soldier who couldn't dodge in time. The soldier was flung far away, landing headfirst.

The horse hit in the abdomen struggled violently, causing more chaos among the soldiers. Taking advantage of the confusion, Adam stealthily approached and fatally stabbed another soldier from behind.

The remaining soldiers finally realized what was happening and charged at Adam with their knives. Quick as lightning, Adam grabbed the reins, leapt onto a horse, and charged at the soldiers, cutting them down. With Timothy's cover from the shadows, the twelve-man team was quickly reduced to two. Blood splattered everywhere, and bodies lay strewn about. Seeing their dire situation, the last two soldiers abandoned the grain carts and fled for their lives.

Adam, disoriented and drenched in blood, slumped off the horse. Timothy, elated, rushed over and gave him a bear hug.

"Adam! We did it!!!"

Adam, his face smeared with blood, stared dazedly at Timothy as he shook his shoulders.

"Yeah, Alan... we did it..."

Adam's face showed a mix of relief and disbelief. He had charged into the fray with a do-or-die attitude and couldn't believe they had succeeded.

Although the process differed from their plan, the grain raid was a resounding success. The news spread through the village, lifting everyone's spirits. When Abbe heard, he was both shocked and delighted. That night, he invited Adam and Timothy to his home, saying he wanted to reward them, and generously brought out his prized wine to celebrate with everyone.

After a few rounds of drinks, Abbe couldn't help but ask, "I examined the site closely. That grain convoy belonged to Penelope, right? Is Rickie running out of grain now?"

Lucas nodded. "With Sunder in drought, Rickie can't escape it. To maintain the luxurious lifestyles of the high officials, Penelope will have to keep bleeding Sunder dry."

Timothy chimed in, "I agree with Uncle. This isn't over. Penelope suffered a loss with land transport and will be more vigilant now. The real prize is in the water transport. We can seize an even bigger opportunity there."

Abbe, hearing this, couldn't help but feel excited.

"Uncle, can I leave this to you?" He turned to Lucas with eager eyes.

Lucas looked at Timothy, then at Abbe, and finally let out a long sigh.

"Chief Master, every time this kid Timothy comes up with some wild idea, you have Uncle handle it! Like the tunnel digging last time. Do you think I'm easy to bully because I'm easygoing?"

Abbe chuckled. "Uncle, this is your specialty. Everyone knows you're the best at gathering intelligence in Sabra Village. No one else can do this job but you."

Lucas knocked Abbe on the head. "Stop taking advantage of me while pretending to be humble!"

"This is not flattery," Timothy chimed in, "Uncle, it's a sign of the Chief Master's reliance on you."

Lucas sighed, pointing at Abbe and Timothy, and said helplessly, "One day, you two kids are going to be the death of me."

Adam, watching from the side in bewilderment, gently nudged Timothy's arm and whispered, "What's with Uncle? He seems like a different person."

Timothy chuckled softly but remained silent.

That night, the group drank until late. Adam, not being able to hold his liquor, was the first to get drunk. With flushed cheeks, he lay in Timothy's arms, mumbling incoherently before falling into a deep sleep. Just as Timothy was about to help Adam back to his room, Abbe called out to him, saying he wanted to have a few words alone with him.

Timothy felt a bit at a loss and looked at Lucas with some concern.

Lucas, sensing the situation, took Adam from Timothy's arms, offering to take him back to his room, implicitly suggesting that Timothy and Abbe should have their talk.

After Lucas left with Adam, the once lively room fell silent.

Abbe took a sip of his wine, and under the candlelight, his downcast eyes and slightly reddened corners revealed a hint of intoxication.

Timothy remained silent, simply watching him until Abbe put down his cup and quietly began to speak. "Timothy, I'm sorry."

Abbe's lips trembled slightly as he continued in a low voice, "I shouldn't have quarreled with you like that. And I definitely shouldn't have scolded you so harshly in front of everyone."

"There's no need for the Chief Master to apologize," Timothy responded calmly. "As the leader of Sabra Village, you have to be responsible for everyone. It's natural to be stricter with an outsider like me."

Abbe looked up and silently gazed at Timothy for a long time before sighing.

"I always thought of myself as a tolerant person, but compared to you, I fall short."

"Chief Master, you're mistaken," Timothy said dismissively, shaking his finger. "I'm quite willful, but I've always been more open-hearted towards beautiful people."

Abbe's face flushed with slight annoyance. "I'm being serious with you!"

"So am I," Timothy replied earnestly.

Abbe stared at Timothy for a while before bursting into laughter.

"The Master is finally smiling," Timothy sighed in relief, smiling as well. "I think the Master looks best when smiling."

"You and your smooth talk," Abbe said, standing up and walking slowly towards Timothy. "Was it really just you and Adam who pulled off today's grain heist?"

"Absolutely," Timothy nodded. "Of course, the main credit goes to Adam. I was just in the background, providing cover with my arrows."

Abbe asked worriedly, "Were you hurt?"

"No, not at all. But Master, you're asking this a bit late, don't you think?" Timothy frowned in mock displeasure. "Why didn't you ask earlier? It made me feel like you didn't care about my well-being."

"In front of everyone, even if I'm concerned, I can't show it too clearly," Abbe replied awkwardly, gently holding Timothy's hand. "Don't be angry."

Timothy's heart skipped a beat. He never expected someone like Abbe to act coyly, and he had to admit, it was quite endearing.

As Abbe held Timothy's hand, he noticed the calluses on his thumb, a testament to Timothy's hard practice in archery over the past few days.

"Your hand..." Abbe murmured.

"It's nothing," Timothy said nonchalantly, smiling as he tried to withdraw his hand, but Abbe held it tightly.

Without a word, Abbe removed a jade ring from his own hand and gently slipped it onto Timothy's thumb. Timothy looked down in surprise and delight; it was the first gift Abbe had ever given him.

"With this, you won't have to worry about hurting your thumb in the future," Abbe said, holding Timothy's hand as if in prayer. "I hope it keeps you safe."

Timothy's heart raced, his mind blank. The usually eloquent and witty Timothy was at a loss for words.

Abbe couldn't see Timothy's expression. He held Timothy's hand for a while longer before reluctantly letting go. "You should go now."

"Huh? Oh..." Timothy snapped out of his daze, realizing that they had been living separately to avoid suspicion. It was late, and he should leave. With a hint of reluctance, he stood up and walked a few steps before stopping to look back at Abbe, wondering if Abbe might change his mind and ask him to stay.

Abbe watched him leave silently, his eyes filled with unspoken words.

After Timothy finally left with a tinge of regret, Abbe sighed softly, barely audibly. "I wish you could be willful just once..."

Of course, Timothy couldn't hear Abbe's words. If he had, he might have stayed.

Instead, that night, he returned to Adam's room. Adam, who had drunk himself into a stupor, lay sprawled out on the bed, dead to the world.

Timothy, exhausted from the day's events, collapsed onto the bed with a slight buzz from the alcohol. The weak candlelight reflected off the jade ring on his thumb, casting a soft glow. Timothy's heart stirred as he gently rubbed the smooth surface of the ring, a faint smile playing on his lips.

Chapter Twenty-One: Cutting Through Thorns

Timothy couldn't remember when he fell asleep.

In the middle of the night, he woke up again with a peculiar sensation, just like last time. This time, however, he didn't open his eyes but instead listened intently and felt what was happening to him with his body.

A hand was gently roaming over his body. Initially, the hand cautiously caressed Timothy's body through his clothes. After a while, seeing no reaction from Timothy, the hand began to slip under his shirt, stroking his chest muscles, with fingers lightly circling his nipples.

Timothy kept his eyes closed, remained silent, and tried his best to keep his breathing steady, as if he were in a deep sleep, showing no reaction to the touch.

However, his body was honest. Soon, his nipples became erect and engorged under the caresses. Timothy's breathing grew heavier, as if he were having a sensual dream, letting out a few helpless murmurs.

The hand paused briefly, but seeing that Timothy hadn't awakened, it grew bolder, starting to slide downwards.

The hand traced the contours of his abs and moved towards Timothy's groin, cautiously grasping his semi-erect member. At the same time, the person's breathing beside him grew heavier, accompanied by the rustling of clothes. It seemed the person was undressing themselves, caressing Timothy's manhood while also satisfying their own desire.

"Mmm..." Before long, the person beside him trembled, moaning as they reached climax in their own hand.

At that moment, Timothy no longer had any doubt that the person was Adam.

Unexpectedly, Adam was indeed using the cover of night to secretly pleasure himself with Timothy's body to relieve his desire.

If Timothy were to open his eyes now, he wondered what expression Adam would have in facing him. One could imagine how panic-stricken he would be.

However, that alone didn't seem to satisfy Adam. After climaxing once, he carefully climbed on top of Timothy. Timothy could feel the sudden weight on his body, suggesting that Adam was straddling him.

Timothy's heart raced, thinking Adam might actually go through with it. Sure enough, Adam leaned over Timothy, placing Timothy's shaft between his buttocks, grinding against him.

Timothy's heart pounded, his groin quickly swelling, his member hardening like hot iron, leaking fluid between Adam's cleft, probing the tightly closed entrance like a thief eager to break in.

Timothy, burning with desire, longed for release but restrained himself, choosing to pretend to be asleep, letting Adam do as he pleased.

After a while of movement on top of Timothy, Adam, seemingly feeling it was time, held Timothy's shaft, positioning the swollen head at his rear entrance.

After much probing, the head finally stretched the tight ring, and Adam, enduring the pain, slowly lowered himself, allowing Timothy's desire to penetrate deeply into the narrow hole.

"Ugh..." With each inch of entry, Adam let out a moan, a mixture of pain and pleasure, sitting on Timothy's abdomen. After adapting to the deeply embedded shaft, Adam bit his lip and began to move up and down.

Timothy, having never experienced such a magical act, lay motionless on the kang bed like a corpse, focusing all his senses on his groin and hearing, creating an unprecedented level of stimulation and pleasure.

Adam started with slow movements but gradually lost himself, moving faster and more freely, until the sloshing sounds of their intimate act echoed in the quiet room, causing their ears to burn with shame.

Unable to contain his curiosity, Timothy opened his eyes slightly, seeing Adam's chest exposed, his hand working on his own member as he moved. Thinking Timothy was unaware, Adam didn't realize his foolishness was being seen clearly by Timothy.

As time went on, Adam struggled to suppress his moans, moving with increasing fervor, sweating profusely, panting heavily, and occasionally letting out restrained, trembling cries.

After around a hundred thrusts, Adam's inner muscles contracted, bringing on a violent tremor. Timothy knew Adam had climaxed again. The sudden, tight grip on his shaft caught Timothy off guard, causing him to ejaculate explosively inside Adam, filling his burning, tight hole.

Adam's body convulsed, letting out a long sigh of pleasure, finally collapsing weakly on Timothy, breathing heavily.

"Alan..." Adam whispered almost inaudibly on Timothy's body.

Timothy remained still. After a long while, he felt two soft lips touch his own.

Adam, cautiously and secretly, brushed his lips against Timothy's, letting his trembling breath fall on Timothy's cheek. After the brief contact, the softness quickly retreated, leaving a lingering warmth on Timothy's lips.

Adam liked Timothy and secretly harbored feelings for him.

For Timothy's feigned sleep, Adam had his own explanation: he believed Timothy had blacked out from drinking, so even though Adam had done such things to him, Timothy remained oblivious.

Thus, when he woke up the next day, Adam acted as if nothing had happened, pretending the night had been uneventful.

Adam clearly didn't want Timothy to know what he had done, thinking he had hidden it well, unaware that Timothy had already seen through his actions. However, Timothy didn't intend to reveal it. After all, he had also enjoyed that night, not feeling wronged. Since Adam didn't bring it up, Timothy didn't want to break the silence, choosing to play along, continuing to be good brothers with him.

Three days later, Lucas, who had sent people to gather information from Rickie, brought back good news.

As Timothy had anticipated, according to informants, Penelope had indeed been gathering food from all over Sunder to transport to Rickie. The main force for transporting the food was the river transportation along River Filat. In the middle of this month, five grain ships carrying 5,000 stones of grain would travel down River Filat to Rickie.

Without delay, upon receiving the news, Abbe immediately gathered Lucas, Timothy, Adam, and a few other trusted generals to discuss the plan to seize the grain. As this operation concerned the survival of all the brothers in Sabra Village, Abbe decided to split the forces into two groups: one led by Lucas to ambush the ships on the shore and cover the main force, and the other led by himself, comprising fifty brothers skilled in swimming, to attack the grain ships from the water.

On the day before the operation, Sunder, which had been suffering from a drought, suddenly experienced a heavy rain, causing temperatures to plummet.

Early the next morning, thick fog enveloped Sabra Village.

"Penelope's grain ships are well-armed and heavily guarded. It won't be easy to seize them," Abbe said solemnly to the crowd gathered before him, "Brothers, today we either succeed or die trying!"

"Either succeed or die trying!"

"To survive, we'll fight to the end!"

Over a thousand Sabra Village brothers echoed passionately, raising their arms and shouting in unison.

Timothy was naturally no exception. Unlike Adam, who had been selected to join Abbe's special attack team, Timothy was assigned to Lucas's unit to ambush on the riverbank and provide cover for Abbe and the others.

A hundred miles northwest of Sabra Village, along River Filat, the heavy rain from the previous night had caused the river to swell. In the thick white fog, Penelope's grain ships slowly approached the ambush site where Lucas, Timothy, and their men lay in wait. On the leading grain ship, a dozen soldiers patrolled the deck, with some lazing about, dozing off against the mast with their weapons.

Suddenly, a sharp whistle pierced through the fog, followed by a rain of arrows shooting towards the grain ships.

"Enemy attack!"

The sharp cry echoed over the river. However, in the thick fog, the soldiers on the ships couldn't see the intruders. Most were struck down by arrows before they could react.

"Take cover!"

With a loud shout, the remaining soldiers hurriedly retreated, some trembling in the ship's cabin, others crouching behind cover, looking around in panic.

Under the cover of a torrential rain of arrows, the underwater special forces team successfully boarded the ship. Abbe was the first to charge into the cabin. At this moment, there were only about thirty surviving soldiers on the ship, completely unaware of the situation and no match for Abbe's fifty deadly warriors. Abbe, decisive and ruthless, swiftly killed more than a dozen soldiers, leaving a trail of blood wherever he went.

The lead ship quickly fell into the hands of Sabra Village—their swift takeover left the following ships unaware of what had transpired ahead.

After all, the fog was incredibly thick.

It wasn't until the bow of the second ship was nearly touching the stern of the first ship that they realized something was wrong. The ship ahead was motionless, eerily silent, with no signs of crew on the deck, as if they had all vanished, turning the vessel into a ghost ship.

What they didn't know was that Abbe, along with fifty brothers who had just completed their task, was lurking underwater, slowly closing in on them.

Once again, a barrage of arrows rained down, followed by a sudden underwater assault. With seamless coordination between Sabra Village's land and water forces, Abbe repeated his earlier tactics, capturing the second ship as well!

However, as the saying goes, things don't always go smoothly. When Abbe attacked the second ship, the sun had risen, and the thick fog was gradually dissipating. The ships behind, noticing something amiss, quickly turned around and sped away.

Even so, capturing two grain ships in one go was an unexpected and tremendous victory for Sabra Village.

However, for Penelope, this was far from a cause for celebration.

"Your Highness King of Nixie!"

That afternoon, the King of Nixie was strolling in his garden with a bird, when Penelope barged in without waiting for the servants to announce her, heading straight to the back garden.

"Isn't this Penelope?" In stark contrast to the furious and fire-breathing Penelope, the King of Nixie was leisurely, smiling as he looked at her and asked, "Why are you so angry?"

"Look at what your subordinates have done!" Penelope said, slamming a confidential letter in front of the King of Nixie. "I've received a spy report saying that your subordinate, Mr. Shaw, has colluded with those rascals in Sabra Village to rob our grain from Sunder! Not once, but twice!!"

The King of Nixie picked up the letter and read it carefully, his brows furrowing slightly.

"Your Highness King of Nixie, Timothy is your subordinate. You must give Penelope an explanation, right!?" Penelope bit her lower lip in anger, staring into the King of Nixie's eyes.

The King of Nixie closed the letter, sighed hypocritically, and feigned regret, "I wondered why Mr. Shaw had been so elusive lately. I never thought, sigh, how could he be so foolish."

At this point, the King of Nixie changed the subject.

"But I am puzzled. How did Mr. Shaw end up in a place like Sabra Village? Penelope, I remember it was you who took him back to the mansion the night of the Mable Banquet, right?"

Facing the King of Nixie's questioning gaze, Penelope froze, quickly shifting her eyes away, "How should I know? After that night, he disappeared without a trace. I never thought... I never thought..."

The more Penelope spoke, the angrier she became, shaking with fury until she finally drew her sword from her waist with a swift motion.

The King of Nixie, seeing this, stepped back nervously, "Penelope, what are you doing?"

Penelope gripped the sword hilt tightly, raised her hand, and with a loud crack, sliced a rock in front of her in half.

With a fierce gleam in her eyes, she growled through gritted teeth, "A bunch of petty thieves dare to mess with me. Timothy, just you wait! I, Penelope, will not let this go unpunished!"

Chapter Twenty-Two: On the Eve of Battle

In the end, Penelope did not get any explanation from the King of Nixie. After all, the King of Nixie was not his subordinate and had his own troops. Unless the King of Nixie personally agreed, he would not easily deploy his forces. The King of Nixie had no intention of clashing with Sabra Village, so he merely brushed off Penelope's questions.

But Penelope was not someone to be easily dismissed. Known for his vengeful nature and resolute actions, he would never swallow this insult silently. Over the next month, Penelope actively recruited and assembled an army of sixty thousand soldiers from all over Sunder. After meticulous preparation, he marched straight towards Sabra Village.

The fierce wind howled, lifting dust and stones. Under the scorching sun, Penelope stood on the observation platform of the mountain opposite Sabra Village, clad in a bright red battle robe. Before him stretched a sea of soldiers, with Morris flags fluttering everywhere, forming a dense formation that surrounded Sabra Village from all sides.

"Timothy..." Penelope bit his lower lip, his eyes flashing with a dark, cold light.

In the past, although the Sunder army had clashed with Sabra Village several times, Penelope had always stayed behind, never personally stepping onto the battlefield. As a result, few in Sabra Village knew what Penelope looked like.

This time was different. Penelope appeared at the front line, wanting everyone to know that this time he meant business.

Facing Penelope's overwhelming force of sixty thousand soldiers, Sabra Village was on high alert.

Abbe knew that with their limited forces, they couldn't confront Penelope head-on. He decided not to engage directly, no matter how Penelope's envoys provoked them. Penelope, on the other hand, wasn't in a hurry. His strategy was clear: he aimed to deplete Sabra Village's supplies, forcing them into a war of attrition to see how long they could hold out on the isolated mountain.

"This won't do," Abbe said one day in the Hall of Heroes, looking around solemnly. "We are outnumbered, and we can't match the Sunder army's supplies."

"Although Penelope seems formidable, he isn't without weaknesses," Lucas said, pointing at the map and explaining the situation. "Penelope has concentrated all his forces at the foot of Sabra Village, trying to surround us. This means his rear must be vulnerable."

Abbe's eyes lit up, and he slapped his thigh. "Perfect! Now the secret tunnel Timothy suggested we build can be put to use."

Lucas nodded. "After over two months of hard work, our brothers have dug a tunnel from the mountain to a dense forest southeast of the village."

"Uncle, what do you suggest we do?" Abbe asked.

"We should send a small, elite force through the tunnel to launch a guerrilla attack on Penelope's rear, disrupting their plans and creating chaos. When the enemy is in disarray, our main forces in the village can concentrate and attack their weak points. This gives us a chance to win."

Lucas's strategy was clear and well thought out, boosting the morale of Abbe and the brothers. The oppressive atmosphere in the village was instantly lifted.

"Alright!" Abbe decided and began to make arrangements.

In the end, Abbe decided to leave Lucas to guard the main camp, while he led one hundred of the bravest warriors down the tunnel to raid Penelope's troops.

Initially, Abbe wanted Timothy to stay at the main camp, but when Timothy learned that Penelope was personally leading the troops, he volunteered to join the raid, insisting he must seize this chance to avenge himself.

"The next part will be close combat," Abbe said, worried. "People will die. Are you up for it?"

Timothy gripped his bow tightly, his eyes blazing. "Chief Master, rest assured! I have been practicing day and night for this moment. I swore to avenge Penelope's attack, and I cannot miss this opportunity!"

Moved by Timothy's determination, Abbe grasped his hand and nodded. "Alright, we go together!"

"Timothy," Lucas said, having quietly approached them.

"Second Master, what are your orders?" Timothy asked respectfully.

Lucas gazed into Timothy's eyes for a long moment, then patted his shoulder. "Take care of Abbe."

Both Timothy and Abbe were surprised and exchanged glances.

Lucas cleared his throat and said softly, "Make sure you bring Abbe back safely."

Timothy, overjoyed by Lucas's trust, responded loudly, "Yes!"

That night, as Penelope was about to lie down in his tent, he suddenly heard a messenger's urgent report.

"What is it? Has Sabra Village mobilized?" Penelope asked anxiously, sitting up.

"Sabra Village remains inactive. It's General Kelly's troops that have been attacked!"

"General Kelly?" Penelope's heart sank. General Kelly's unit was closest to the granary. "Who attacked?"

"A group of masked men in black, about a hundred strong."

"Could it be reinforcements for Sabra Village?" Penelope stood up, pacing the tent in deep thought before shaking his head. "Impossible. I've never heard of them allying with any other force. How could they have reinforcements?"

Now was not the time to dwell on such details. Penelope immediately dispatched two units, totaling five thousand men, from the base of Sabra Village. One unit went to assist General Kelly, and the other to reinforce the granary.

The raiders, led by Abbe and Timothy, set fire to the camp as soon as they charged in. It was a dry season, and the flames quickly spread. General Kelly's soldiers, thinking they were under a large-scale attack, couldn't distinguish friend from foe in the chaos. Cries, curses, and the sounds of battle filled the air. Many Sunder soldiers fell not to Abbe's men but to friendly fire or were trampled underfoot in the confusion.

Abbe fought fearlessly, leading the charge and taking down multiple enemies with swift, decisive moves.

At that moment, a soldier with a spear suddenly emerged from the shadows, charging at Abbe's back. From several paces behind, Timothy quickly drew his bow and shot an arrow that pierced the soldier's neck.

"Timothy!?" Abbe turned around, both surprised and delighted.

"Chief Master!" Timothy ran forward, grabbing Abbe's hand.

Unlike the hot-headed Abbe, Timothy was cautious and methodical, always staying close to Abbe to protect him. After all, Abbe was the backbone of Sabra Village, and his loss would be devastating.

"You know how dangerous that was!" Timothy scolded Abbe for the first time, genuinely worried and unable to hold back.

"Sorry, I lose my head in battle!" Abbe chuckled.

Timothy sighed. "I know you're strong, but please, be more careful."

Seeing the concern on Timothy's face, Abbe felt a warm sensation in his heart and said softly, "I have you, don't I?"

Timothy was taken aback. "What did you say?"

"Nothing!" Abbe grabbed Timothy's hand. "Let's talk later. Time to retreat before Penelope's reinforcements arrive!"

With that, Abbe whistled sharply, and he, Timothy, and their men quickly withdrew, leaving behind a scene of chaos and corpses for Penelope.

Seeing Abbe and Timothy's successful raid not only caught Penelope off guard but also brought back all fifty warriors unharmed, lifting the morale of Sabra Village.

When Penelope learned of the raid, he was furious, slamming his fist on the table. By the time his reinforcements arrived, the attackers had vanished, leaving Penelope's forces thoroughly humiliated.

Yet this was merely the beginning. Over the next week, Abbe's elite guerrilla force continued to harass Penelope's rear, striking here today and there tomorrow, always vanishing without a trace after causing chaos. To capture Abbe and Timothy, Penelope had to constantly redeploy his troops, rushing from one crisis to another.

Of course, so far, Abbe and Timothy's raids hadn't dealt a fatal blow to the Sunder army. After all, Penelope still commanded a formidable force of forty thousand men, meaning his main strength was intact.

One day, back in the village, Abbe visited the training grounds where the brothers were practicing. Hearing about the guerrilla force's repeated victories, the morale was high, and everyone eagerly requested to join the battle.

"Chief Master, now is the perfect time for us to launch a frontal assault," Lucas advised Abbe. "Recent defeats at the rear have demoralized the Sunder troops. This is our chance to break through their lines."

"But Penelope is a cunning old fox," Abbe mused. "We've wreaked havoc on his rear, yet he remains holed up in his main camp, refusing to come out. To end this quickly, we must lure him out and capture him."

"To lure Penelope out? That's easy."

Timothy, who usually stayed silent during tactical discussions, suddenly spoke up.

"Timothy?" Abbe looked at him in surprise. "What do you suggest?"

"We just need to send someone to the enemy camp," Timothy said, his eyes gleaming.

"Who?" Abbe asked.

"Me," Timothy replied calmly.

"You? Alone, to see Penelope?" Abbe was stunned, doubting he had heard correctly.

"Timothy, what are you planning?" Even Lucas, usually quick-witted, was puzzled.

"It's simple. I go alone to Penelope's camp and draw him out," Timothy explained.

"That's too dangerous!" Abbe was the first to object. "It's like walking into the lion's den! What if Penelope kills you on sight?"

"That's a possibility," Timothy admitted.

"You..." Abbe was completely taken aback.

"Haha, just kidding," Timothy said with a casual laugh. "Don't worry, Penelope wouldn't dare kill me."

"Why not?" Abbe asked, unable to comprehend.

Because I'm a court official, Timothy thought, but he couldn't say that out loud. Instead, he said, "To deal with someone as suspicious as Penelope, you must act openly. If he sees me entering his camp alone, he'll suspect a trap and won't act rashly."

"That's true, but how will you lure him out?" Abbe asked, still hesitant.

Timothy smiled slightly. "I have my ways."

Abbe looked at Timothy, his expression full of uncertainty.

"Chief Master, Timothy is clever. I think his plan is worth trying," Lucas said.

"Even you, uncle?" Abbe frowned in frustration.

"Yes, Chief Master, trust me this once," Timothy said, winking at Abbe.

Abbe pondered for a long time before reluctantly agreeing.

Although Abbe agreed, he was uneasy about Timothy going to the enemy camp alone. Since the war began, he and Timothy had always fought on the front lines together. Even when Timothy wasn't in his direct line of sight, Abbe could sense his presence nearby, giving him an indescribable sense of security.

Strangely, despite his own courage and fearlessness, Abbe had come to rely on Timothy's presence. The thought of Timothy leaving him made Abbe uncomfortable. It wasn't that he didn't trust Timothy; it was just a feeling of unease that something bad might happen.

Timothy, however, was full of confidence. The day before his departure, he trained late into the night, and Abbe, watching from the sidelines, couldn't bring himself to stop him.

Timothy's progress was evident. Since coming to Sabra Village, his archery had improved significantly. While not yet able to hit a target at one hundred paces, he had developed considerable strength and accuracy.

So what was Abbe worried about?

He couldn't answer his own question.

"Master!" Timothy, shirtless and drenched in sweat, ran up to Abbe in the nearly deserted training ground. "You're here! Why didn't you say something earlier?"

Abbe handed him a dry cloth. "I saw you were so focused, I didn't want to interrupt. You have an important task tomorrow; you should rest instead of overexerting yourself."

Timothy smiled dismissively. "I know my limits. I'll be fine."

Abbe sighed softly. "Always saying you know your limits... What are you really thinking?"

"Master? What did you say?" Timothy pretended not to hear and leaned closer.

"You stink!" Abbe grimaced, pinching his nose. "When was the last time you bathed?"

"Let me think..." Timothy scratched his head, trying to remember.

Abbe had enough and grabbed his ear. "Enough thinking! Go take a bath!"

Timothy, pushed by Abbe, jumped into a large tub of icy well water, shivering as the cold hit him.

Leaning against the tub, Timothy let Abbe wash the grime from his hair, feeling the gentle pressure of Abbe's fingertips on his scalp.

They chatted casually about their battles against Penelope and archery techniques. Timothy's lively chatter filled the air, and Abbe listened with a smile, suddenly realizing Timothy had gone quiet. He looked up to find Timothy staring intently at him.

"What did you say?" Abbe asked, thinking Timothy was waiting for a response.

"Master, your ears are really beautiful," Timothy said.

"Ears?" Abbe was taken aback. Before he could react, Timothy reached out and pinched his left earlobe.

Abbe shuddered. Timothy's fingers gently kneaded his earlobe, the rough texture of his fingertips gliding over the soft flesh.

"Round and full," Timothy murmured with a low laugh. "I wonder how they taste."

It was a strange feeling, hard to describe. Abbe had always been sensitive about his ears, hating when anyone touched them. Yet, Timothy was an exception.

"Don't... don't touch them..." Abbe's voice trembled, uncharacteristically soft and embarrassed.

Timothy paused, and Abbe's face flushed. He pushed Timothy away, covering his ears, his heart racing.

"Master..." Timothy, thinking he had overstepped, stood up quickly, splashing water everywhere and exposing himself to Abbe.

Though Abbe had seen plenty of men naked, he felt a sudden rush of embarrassment, pushing Timothy back.

"Whoa...!"

Timothy, unsteady on his feet, swayed back and forth in the bathtub, helplessly grabbing onto Abbe, followed by a loud crash.

The bathtub overturned, water splashed everywhere, and Abbe found himself pinned beneath a naked Timothy, soaked to the skin.

Timothy hadn't expected Abbe's ears to be so sensitive to touch.

Because it was only when their bodies were pressed together, face to face, that Timothy noticed a bulge in Abbe's crotch.

Neither of them spoke. The room was filled with an awkward and ambiguous silence. But at the same time, their tightly pressed chests housed hearts that were pounding fiercely, drumming like a battle cry.

Finally, Timothy broke the silence, swallowing hard, "Master, you're hard."

"Who told you to touch me?"

Abbe bit his lower lip, but his ears were so red they seemed ready to bleed. Seeing this, Timothy's mischievous side emerged, and he lowered his head to lightly brush Abbe's earlobe with his hot tongue.

"Ah...!" Abbe couldn't suppress a moan.

Surprised by Abbe's sensitivity, Timothy decided to fully envelop that earlobe in his mouth. The moment it entered, Abbe's body shuddered involuntarily beneath him.

"Delicious..." Timothy rasped in Abbe's ear, gently nibbling on the soft flesh with his teeth.

"Stop... stop..." Abbe's body finally began to tremble uncontrollably, his lower abdomen twitching, the bulge in his groin swollen to the point of bursting.

"Timothy...!" Abbe's tears of discomfort spilled over as he weakly pushed against Timothy's chest. Seeing him in such a state, Timothy could no longer hold back. He quickly reached down to unfasten Abbe's belt, pulling his pants down.

"What... what are you doing?" Abbe asked in confusion.

"Helping my master release some tension." Timothy said, caressing the smooth, white skin of Abbe's inner thigh. "And perhaps my master can lend his body to relieve his disciple too."

With that, Timothy pulled Abbe into his embrace, sliding his hand down to grasp the already erect member, while pressing his own hardness between Abbe's thighs, moving both his hand and hips in unison.

Abbe had never experienced anything like this before; he felt like a fish on a chopping block, flopping between life and death, teetering on the edge of pain and pleasure. He suddenly remembered the conversations he used to have with the village brothers, some of whom were into this sort of thing, and he had a rough idea of what went on between men. But he never thought such a thing would happen to him, let alone with Timothy.

Yet, despite knowing they were doing something shameful, his body didn't reject Timothy's advances. Instead, it became more excited under Timothy's caresses.

In a muddled state, Abbe turned his head, meeting Timothy's eager eyes.

In that moment, Abbe felt as if Timothy's gaze would consume him entirely.

Before he realized it, Abbe found himself kissing Timothy passionately. Their lips and tongues entwined deeply, Abbe's hand instinctively reaching to the back of Timothy's head, pulling him closer.

With a thud, the bathtub was kicked aside, rolling across the wet floor and knocking over a vase on a cabinet, which shattered upon impact.

Startled, Timothy instinctively shielded Abbe with his body, fearing someone had entered. Abbe, leaning into Timothy's embrace, saw the door wide open, but no one was there, only the door swaying in the wind, creaking ominously.

The sudden scare was like a cold shower, quenching their desire and bringing them back to reality.

"What now... the fire is already out."

Timothy said dejectedly. Abbe glanced down, and they exchanged looks, then burst into laughter.

"What are you standing around for? Get up!"

Abbe said, both amused and exasperated. Timothy sheepishly got up and dressed. Abbe quickly put on his pants, calming his racing heart and tidying himself up.

Although their moment was interrupted, the feelings were already deeply rooted.

After dressing, Timothy said, "Wait here," and ran out of the room. Abbe, puzzled, waited anxiously until Timothy returned with something in his hands.

"Master, I want to give you something."

Timothy said, opening his hand to reveal a pair of exquisite love bean earrings.

Abbe's eyes widened in disbelief, "These are for me?"

"Consider it a token of appreciation for the jade ring." Timothy smiled shyly, "They're not worth much, but when I first saw them, they reminded me of you."

"Reminded you of me?" Abbe's heart fluttered, but he hesitated, "But I don't have pierced ears..."

"I'll pierce them for you." Timothy volunteered, "Don't worry, it won't hurt."

"Really?" Abbe was skeptical, "How do you do it?"

"It's simple."

Timothy wasted no time. He heated a silver needle over a candle flame, then placed two small grains of rice between his thumb and forefinger. He gently lifted Abbe's hair, holding his earlobe between the rice grains, rubbing it softly.

As Timothy's fingers touched his earlobe, Abbe's heart leaped to his throat again. Despite the earlier antics, Abbe seemed to have gotten somewhat used to Timothy's handling, but his body still trembled involuntarily.

Once the earlobe was sufficiently thinned, Timothy took the red-hot needle and pierced Abbe's earlobe.

Suddenly, a sharp pain shot through his earlobe, and Abbe let out a small gasp, but the pain quickly subsided.

"See? I told you it wouldn't hurt much, right, Master?" Timothy grinned.

"It wasn't as bad as I thought." Abbe sighed in relief.

Timothy repeated the process on Abbe's other earlobe, then carefully placed the love bean earrings.

"They look nice." Abbe said, looking at himself in the mirror, though his eyebrows furrowed, "But... it feels strange."

"Strange how?" Timothy asked.

"I can't quite explain it." Abbe said softly, touching his earlobes, "It feels like I've lost something important."

Timothy chuckled, leaning down to quickly flick his tongue over the little red dot on Abbe's earlobe, "Oh? Lost your innocence, perhaps?"

Abbe shivered and turned to playfully scold him, "You cheeky!"

"Seriously though," Timothy said earnestly, "Wearing these means that Abbe belongs to me now."

Abbe's heart raced as he met Timothy's intense gaze, recalling their earlier passionate moments. His thoughts were tangled, just like the night sounds outside and the lingering iron scent in the air, which seemed to transform into a sweet catalyst.

Summoning a sudden burst of courage, Abbe wrapped his arms around Timothy's neck, quickly planting a kiss on his lips.

"When you return, we'll continue where we left off..."

Chapter Twenty-Three: A Lone Rider Enters the Fray

Early the next morning, led by Abbe, the people of Sabra Village reluctantly bid farewell to Timothy at the village gate.

Lucas, like an old father, kept babbling on, while Adam seemed to have had a sleepless night, with his eyes slightly swollen. As for Abbe, he indeed wore the love token Timothy had given him the day before—earrings made of red beans. Perhaps still unaccustomed to the foreign object on his ears, he kept unconsciously reaching up to rub his earlobes while talking.

The weather changed its face as quickly as flipping a page. What had been a clear sky yesterday turned into a thick layer of dark clouds hovering close to the horizon, signaling an impending storm. In such a scene, who wouldn't be moved by the melancholy of "the wind is cold and the water is chilly"?

However, Timothy was clearly not among them. Despite bearing Abbe's concern, Adam's worry, and Lucas's trust, Timothy remained calm. Under the watchful eyes of the villagers, he rode out of Sabra Village alone, gracefully descending the mountain.

No sooner had he reached the foot of the mountain than he was surrounded by a group of soldiers who had been lying in wait.

The soldiers, seeing a lone rider without any weapons or heavy armor, and with an unflappable demeanor, were puzzled. While they were exchanging confused glances, Timothy slowly began to speak.

"Tell your commander, Penelope, that Timothy requests an audience."

After a while, the order came from the back of the army, delivered by Penelope herself: Let him in, do not hinder.

Thus, under the gaze of countless eyes, Timothy swaggered up to Penelope's tent.

Penelope, clad in armor, sat on a tall horse, a spear held across her front.

"Penelope, long time no see. You're as striking as ever," Timothy reined in his horse several yards away, looking around at the well-prepared troops. "But judging by your setup, this doesn't seem like a welcome for an old friend."

"We're not old friends!" Penelope's eyebrows furrowed as she slammed her spear to the ground. "Cut the crap! What are you here for? Speak honestly, or I'll have your head!"

"Don't be so harsh, you'll get wrinkles," Timothy responded with a roguish smile. "I came here to surrender. I'm not asking for a grand reception, but at least don't put on such a menacing display."

"Surrender?" Penelope narrowed her eyes suspiciously, scrutinizing Timothy.

"Don't believe me?" Seeing Penelope's guarded expression, Timothy sighed. "Come closer, it's tiring to shout from so far away."

After carefully examining Timothy again and seeing that he came alone and unarmed, Penelope felt slightly reassured and urged her horse forward slowly.

"What are you up to?" Penelope asked in a low voice, eyes locked on Timothy's.

"Up to something?" Timothy laughed. "If we're talking about schemes, how could I show off in front of you, Penelope? You know very well what you did to me back then."

"Oh? So you're here to settle scores?" Penelope snorted.

"Don't lump me with petty people like you," Timothy smiled. "I stole your supplies, killed your men, and broke your spirit. That settled my grudge. Our past grievances are over."

"You say it's over? Clearly, you took advantage of me!" Penelope pointed at Timothy angrily. "Don't forget what you did to me at Mervyn!"

"Ah, that?" Timothy leaned closer and put an arm around Penelope's shoulders. "It was just a kiss."

"You... let go!!" Penelope, red with anger, tried to push Timothy away but couldn't match his strength.

Penelope was flustered, but to the surrounding soldiers, it looked like something entirely different—their commander and Timothy's horses stood neck to neck, with Timothy intimately holding their commander, whispering secrets.

The soldiers exchanged confused glances, unsure of the situation or what to do.

Timothy continued to grin mischievously. "Stop pretending to be so virtuous, Penelope. You've done more shameless things in public. I just slipped and kissed you. What's the big deal?"

"That's different!" Penelope retorted.

"Really? And that night when you got me drunk and took advantage of me? Didn't you touch me inappropriately?" Timothy persisted.

Penelope, hit on a sore spot, bit her lip. "Fine! Let's say I owe you. Are you done? Let go!"

"No way. I didn't come here to argue, and I haven't achieved my goal yet," Timothy said, his eyes flashing as he leaned closer. "Withdraw your troops, Penelope."

"What?" Penelope was stunned, unable to believe her ears. "What nonsense are you spouting? You want me to withdraw?"

"Of course not nonsense. Let me be straightforward. I came from Poiema to Sunder, not just as a military inspector, but to recruit a brave and strong force for the emperor back in Poiema. That force is Sabra Village."

Penelope was shocked. As an experienced official, he instantly grasped Timothy's meaning. Penelope scrutinized Timothy again, as if seeing him for the first time.

"You, a mere inspector... have quite the guts."

"Are you impressed?" Timothy smiled, touching his nose. "I was born to do great things."

"I'm not complimenting you," Penelope rolled his eyes.

"You're besieging Sabra Village with six thousand troops just to vent your anger. Even if you level Sabra Village, what's the point? A man should achieve great deeds. I've already convinced the King of Nixie to join me in a grand plan. If you join us, the combined forces of three powers will ensure success."

Penelope squinted, staring at Timothy for a long time before speaking in a deep voice. "What if I refuse?"

"Then we fight to the death," Timothy replied nonchalantly.

"Here?" Penelope scoffed. "You, alone and unarmed, against my thousands of soldiers? Fight to the death?"

"Why not? If you dare lay a hand on me, I'll make sure you go down with me. I don't care if I die, Abbe and the others will avenge me, and the King of Nixie will continue my mission. But if you die, your army will lose its leader and soon crumble. In battle, who do you think will win—Sabra Village's united forces or your demoralized troops?"

Penelope was speechless. Seeing Timothy's calm demeanor, he couldn't help but doubt if Timothy had reinforcements hidden nearby.

After a long silence, Penelope finally waved his hand, ordering the troops to withdraw.

"A gamble, huh?" Penelope raised his eyebrows defiantly, meeting Timothy's gaze. "Penelope accepts the challenge!"

Upon returning to the camp, Penelope sat at her desk and penned a peace letter with swift strokes. The content was concise and dignified, clearly stating the intention to negotiate peace and setting a meeting at noon the next day by the River Filat to discuss the truce. Timothy, confirming the letter, was about to head back when Penelope stopped him.

"Wait," Penelope said, rising from the desk and calling for a messenger. "Take this peace letter to Sabra Village and hand it to Abbe."

The messenger took the letter and quickly departed.

Timothy, not understanding, watched Penelope approach him slowly, raising an eyebrow as he spoke softly, "Why leave now that you're here, brother?"

Sensing something amiss in Penelope's tone, Timothy smirked, "What scheme are you up to this time? I'm not the same Timothy who first arrived in Sunder. I won't fall for your tricks again."

Penelope's face turned cold immediately, "I'm not a mind reader. You talk sweetly, but who knows if you'll break the alliance the moment you turn around and catch me off guard?"

So, Penelope intended to hold him as a hostage.

Timothy sighed with a helpless smile, "Do you take me, Timothy, for someone who breaks promises?"

Penelope lifted her chin, "One should always have a fallback."

"Such a petty mind. Your own heart is dirty, so you see everything as dirty," Timothy shrugged. "Fine, I have a clear conscience. I'll stay. What are you planning to do with me? Chain me up? Throw me in a cell?"

"Don't be in such a rush. You'll know by tomorrow," Penelope yawned deliberately, looking exhausted. "These days, being toyed with by Sabra Village has left me sleepless. My head is spinning, I just can't take it..."

Before he finished speaking, Penelope staggered and leaned weakly against Timothy's chest.

"Hey!!" Timothy reflexively supported Penelope's shoulders. Despite his protests, Penelope remained silent, soon snoring softly.

Timothy didn't expect Penelope to fall asleep on him. He called for assistance, but no one answered. After a moment of hesitation, seeing no signs of Penelope waking up, he had to carry Penelope to the soft couch inside.

Maybe it was the result of his recent archery practice, but Timothy didn't find it too hard to carry Penelope, a grown man. What puzzled him was that even in sleep, Penelope's hand reached out to clasp Timothy's neck. Glancing down, Timothy saw Penelope's eyes closed, long lashes still, and lips moving slightly as if mumbling in a dream.

Suspecting Penelope was faking sleep to test his sincerity, Timothy chuckled inwardly. He wondered what would happen if he dropped Penelope to the ground.

"Stop pretending. I know you're faking," Timothy smirked. "If you don't wake up, I'll let go."

Penelope didn't respond, but his hand gripped a lock of Timothy's hair.

"Ouch, ouch! Let go, let go!"

Timothy winced in pain, "Okay, okay, I won't drop you."

Penelope nestled against Timothy, a barely perceptible smile on his lips.

Timothy had no choice but to gently place Penelope on the couch. Lying there quietly, Penelope's long hair spread like a waterfall. At this moment, with his fox-like eyes closed and his sharp tongue silent, Penelope seemed less annoying.

Timothy finally had the chance to admire Penelope's handsome face. He thought how nice it would be if Penelope could always be this way, finding it hard to look away.

Penelope forgot when he fell asleep. Initially, he planned to test Timothy by pretending to sleep, but the sleepless nights caught up with him. Once he closed his eyes, drowsiness overcame him, and he drifted off. When he opened his eyes again, it was night.

Penelope broke out in a cold sweat, quickly sitting up to find Timothy dozing nearby, propping his chin on his hand. Timothy, a light sleeper, woke at the slightest sound, yawning as he looked at Penelope, "Finally awake?"

Penelope tried to suppress his panic, smoothing his slightly disheveled hair, "How long did I sleep?"

"Three hours," Timothy smiled. "As a commander, sleeping like this in front of someone you don't trust is a major mistake."

Penelope gritted his teeth, feeling deep regret. He knew better than to let his guard down around Timothy. If Timothy had harbored any ill intent, Penelope might have been dead by now.

"I suppose I should thank you for sparing my life."

Penelope quickly composed himself. Just then, a messenger arrived with a letter from Abbe. Timothy's eyes lit up as he stood, "What does Abbe say? Let me see!"

Penelope glanced at the letter, his expression tightening slightly before tossing it to Timothy, "See for yourself."

Timothy eagerly read the letter, blushing at the sight of the bold characters: "Meet at noon tomorrow by River Filat." Following the large characters was a hasty addition: "If you dare harm Timothy, I, Abbe, will make you pay!"

The large characters, written in a bold and round hand, were clearly by Lucas, while the smaller, hasty addition was unmistakably Abbe's.

Penelope sneered, "Seems like someone is always thinking of you, no matter where you go."

Timothy chuckled, "I may not have many virtues, but I do have good friends."

"Friends? It seems more than that," Penelope said with a hint of jealousy. "This Master Simpson seems to have a special place for you."

Just as Timothy was about to respond, his stomach growled loudly.

Penelope couldn't help but laugh, clapping his hands to summon the cook. Soon, a lavish meal and several bottles of fine wine were brought in.

With the food scarcity in Sabra Village, Timothy hadn't had a proper meal in days. Seeing the feast before him, he couldn't help but drool. He didn't stand on ceremony, digging in heartily while silently appreciating the difference between Penelope's privileged life and his own.

"Look at you, wolfing it down," Penelope teased, pouring wine into Timothy's cup. "I bet your talk of peace was just an excuse to leave that miserable place, wasn't it?"

"Don't lump me with someone who despises the poor," Timothy said between bites. "The brothers in Sabra Village treated me well, and as for Abbe..."

At the mention of Abbe, Timothy's tone softened, his mind filling with images of Abbe's spirited face. He smiled involuntarily.

"I would never betray him," Timothy said to himself.

Penelope's hand paused, lifting his eyes to silently watch Timothy for a long time.

"Hey! The wine is spilling!"

It was Timothy's sudden exclamation that snapped Penelope out of his daze. Lost in thought, he had unwittingly spilled the wine, drenching Timothy.

"What were you thinking about?" Timothy glanced at him sideways, "So lost in thought."

Penelope quickly leaned over, using his sleeve to wipe Timothy's clothes, murmuring, "It's nothing."

"Penelope, you are acting really strange today... mm!?"
Halfway through his sentence, Timothy abruptly stopped, his expression turning inexplicably strange.
He wasn't the only one with a strange expression. Under the candlelight, Penelope's dark pupils were slowly widening, and his mouth twitched slightly. At this moment, his hand was inadvertently pressing against Timothy's dampened crotch, feeling something that definitely shouldn't have been there.

Chapter Twenty-Four: Sudden Changes

"Aren't you a eunuch!?" Penelope, furious and embarrassed, grabbed Timothy by the collar. "How can you have... this!?"

Timothy looked innocent, "You didn't know? I thought you discovered my secret when you touched me all over after I got drunk that night..."

Penelope, blushing, retorted, "I was just helping you change clothes because you threw up on both of us! Do you think I really lust after your body!?"

"Really?" Timothy was half-convinced. He was very drunk that night but not so much that he couldn't remember. He distinctly recalled those hands lingering on his chest for quite some time.

"Stop changing the subject!" Penelope drew the sword from his waist and pointed it at Timothy. "Tell me, who are you really? Why are you pretending to be a eunuch? If you don't give me a satisfactory explanation, I'll execute you on the spot and report it to the court!"

"Alright, alright! I'll tell you..." Timothy's mind raced as he concocted a new version of his entry into the palace. This time, he completely omitted Christopher, fabricating a story about how Queen Owen recruited handsome young men from outside the palace, including himself. To avoid being used by Queen Owen, he disguised himself as a newly admitted eunuch. Queen Owen, impressed by his looks and cleverness, kept him close as a personal attendant.

At first, Penelope was skeptical, but as Timothy recounted the Queen's misdeeds in the harem, Penelope had to believe him.

Timothy grew more animated, describing his perilous experiences with the enthusiasm of a storyteller, saliva flying as he spoke. Penelope, initially stunned, grew increasingly grim, his forehead veins bulging.

"Outrageous!" Penelope, furious, raised his hand and sliced off a corner of the table in front of Timothy. "Our Great Alvah will fall to this scourge sooner or later!"

Timothy was surprised, "Are you really the young marquis who swore the Oath of Allegiance to Sabra Village?"

Penelope, realizing his outburst, composed himself and asked, "What do you mean?"

"I thought noblemen like you only cared about pleasure and your own comfort. I didn't expect you to have a sense of righteousness," Timothy said, reaching out to touch Penelope's forehead. "No fever?"

Blushing, Penelope slapped Timothy's hand away, "My family has been loyal to the throne for generations. What's so strange about that?"

"True." Timothy nodded, "Your grandfather did help the founding emperor establish the kingdom."

Penelope snorted, "If it weren't for our family's support, Great Alvah wouldn't have stabilized so quickly! Given our family's contributions, it's only right to enjoy some benefits."

Timothy was speechless. It was the first time he'd seen someone justify such crooked reasoning so righteously.

However, Penelope's stance reassured Timothy. It seemed King of Nixie's prediction was correct. As long as the peace talks the next day went smoothly, Sabra Village and Sunder's forces could reconcile, and Timothy would gain two powerful allies, achieving his mission in Sunder.

Fortune indeed favored him, Timothy thought. Being "exiled" to this remote place by Queen Owen had also opened another door for him, bringing him closer to his goals.

Feeling elated, and with Penelope continuously offering wine, Timothy drank cup after cup, gradually losing consciousness.

Drunkenly, Timothy mistook Penelope for Christopher and began talking nonsense, hugging him tightly.

"Your Majesty, wait for me... hic!" Timothy slurred, "I'll... hic... come back to save... you..."

"Brother, you have the wrong person," Penelope whispered in Timothy's ear, "I am Penelope."

"Penelope?" Timothy looked up, staring at him for a moment, then laughed, "No, you're Master..."

Penelope smiled faintly, saying nothing, realizing that Timothy was completely out of his senses.

Timothy continued to mumble incoherently, hugging Penelope tightly, until he finally fell silent and began snoring lightly. Meanwhile, Penelope discreetly brushed away a small pile of powder from the table with a flick of his sleeve.

The next day at noon, by the River Filat.

The two armies faced each other across the river. On the east bank were Penelope's Sunder soldiers, and on the west bank were Abbe's men from Sabra Village. A small boat floated on the river, with Penelope standing alone at the bow.

Abbe and Lucas rowed to the center of the river, stopping before Penelope's boat.

"Where's Timothy?" Abbe asked warily, looking around. "Why didn't he come with you?"

"He drank too much last night. He's still lying on the couch, unable to get up," Penelope replied nonchalantly. "Forget about him. The truce concerns our two armies. Only you and I can make decisions. He's just an outsider."

Abbe frowned but said nothing.

Once Abbe and Lucas boarded the boat, Penelope signaled his men to hand a letter to Abbe.

"I know you don't want to waste words with me, so I'll get straight to the point. Abbe, if you're willing to lead Sabra Village to surrender to Sunder, I assure you that you will not be mistreated. Not just you, but also your advisor here and all the men of Sabra Village. I promise high positions and great wealth."

Abbe's face changed drastically as he read the letter.

"Penelope... are you joking!?" Abbe, trembling with anger, crumpled the letter and threw it at Penelope's face. "Are you insulting me!?"

The ball of paper bounced off Penelope's forehead and fell to the ground. His expression darkened, lips pressed into a thin line as he stared silently at Abbe.

"Yesterday, you gave me a letter proposing peace! Peace! A truce! Not surrender!" Abbe pointed at Penelope's nose. "I'm not here to hear your empty promises or to seek high positions and great wealth! If you have no intention of a truce, we have nothing to talk about!"

Penelope glared at Abbe, silent for a long time before laughing bitterly.

"Master Simpson, I advise you not to be so selfish."

"Selfish?" Abbe was puzzled.

"Isn't it?" Penelope opened a sandalwood fan, fanning himself nonchalantly. "Which is better for Sabra Village, a truce or surrender? You must know."

Abbe gritted his teeth, saying nothing.

"If it's just a truce, Sabra Village will soon be isolated and helpless due to a lack of supplies. Even if you manage to get enough food, without a strong backing, you'll always be a group of displaced people, eventually forced to beg. As the master, you might not starve first, but what about your men? They have families, parents, and children. Who will take care of them? Can you provide for them?"

Seeing Abbe and Lucas exchange silent glances, Penelope continued, "But I can. If you surrender, I'll ensure your men live well, with riches and comfort, getting what they could never dream of. Whether it's fame, status, or beautiful companions, whatever they want, I can give. The only difference is that they won't follow you anymore. With such generous terms, why refuse? If not for selfishness, what else?"

"You're wrong! The men of Sabra Village don't follow Chief Master for money or fame," Lucas finally spoke up. "We follow him because we trust him, knowing he's the only one who treats us as his own."

Penelope sneered, "Really? Mr. Ward, such noble sentiments are admirable, but what about your men? Making decisions for them without asking, is that right?"

Lucas, with righteous indignation, replied, "I know they feel the same! We only recognize Chief Master and will follow him for life!"

"Uncle..." Abbe's eyes reddened with emotion.

"Chief Master, it seems there's no point in saying more. Since Penelope has no intention of peace, why should we stay here?"

"Indeed!" Abbe nodded, turning to glare at Penelope. "Never speak of surrender again. We'll settle this honorably on the battlefield. Whether victor or vanquished, I, Abbe, will have no complaints!"

With that, Abbe turned to leave with Lucas.

But as soon as he turned, dozens of dark shadows leapt from the River Filat, and in a flash, a cold light slashed toward Abbe's back. Lucas shouted, "Chief Master! Watch out!" and with a thud, he grabbed Abbe and fell into the river. Blood spread across the water in moments.

Abbe, holding the now still Lucas, struggled desperately toward the shore. As he moved, the sounds of battle erupted on land. Soldiers surged from all directions, encircling the men of Sabra Village. The villagers were completely taken by surprise, not knowing what had happened. In the blink of an eye, their Chief Master Abbe and advisor Lucas had disappeared.

Adam, with sharp eyes, saw Abbe struggling in the water and shouted, "Chief Master is in the river! Save him!"

Several skilled swimmers dove into the river to rescue Abbe, while Adam stood on the shore, yelling at Penelope, "Penelope! You despicable scoundrel! You had no intention of peace! You planned this ambush from the start to annihilate us!"

"Your Chief Master brought this upon himself, refusing my generous offer," Penelope responded coldly, addressing the men of Sabra Village. "Had he accepted my terms, you all could have joined me, enjoying wealth and honor in Rickie."

The men of Sabra Village were in an uproar.

With the help of his comrades, Abbe finally dragged Lucas ashore. He cradled Lucas, desperately slapping his face and calling his name. Lucas, pale as death, eyes closed, was barely breathing. A deep arrow wound in his left chest poured blood, staining him red.

"Uncle... don't scare Abbe... wake up!" Abbe's voice trembled as he cried, his face streaked with tears. He frantically tried to stop the bleeding, but the blood wouldn't stop, soon covering his hands in red.

Tears the size of beans rolled down onto Lucas's face. Lucas opened his eyes with great effort and whispered, "Abbe... Uncle... can't stay with you..."

"No! No!" Abbe, pressing on Lucas's wound, shook his head wildly, tears falling from his eyes. "You will live a long life! You will always be with Abbe! You won't leave!"

Lucas, with a faint smile, said softly, "Abbe, live well..."

All of Abbe's efforts were in vain. Realizing his helplessness, he broke down in tears, unable to speak, clinging to Lucas's neck as if refusing to let him go.

A rumble of thunder sounded in the oppressive silence, and raindrops began to fall at Abbe's feet. It was as if the heavens mourned this parting. The rain gradually increased, and as it poured, Lucas took his last breath in Abbe's arms.

No one moved. Not the men of Sabra Village, nor the soldiers of Sunder.

The Sunder soldiers remained still because Penelope had not given an order, while the men of Sabra Village were paralyzed with confusion. Their advisor Lucas was dead, their Chief Master Abbe was weeping, and their enemy's leader, Penelope, had just extended an olive branch.

No one knew what to do.

Finally, Penelope broke the silence, dealing the final blow to Abbe's spirit.

"Mr. Ward was right, isn't it better to live? Why seek death? Surrender, Abbe. Without Mr. Ward, you still have Timothy, don't you?"

Hearing Timothy's name, Abbe froze, murmuring to himself, "Yes, Timothy... where is he? What have you done to him!?"

"What have I done?" Penelope chuckled, "It's absurd. Do you think I would dare harm an official of the court?"

"An official... of the court?" Abbe looked bewildered.

"Ah, you're still in the dark?" Penelope's face finally showed a satisfied smile. "The surrender plan was Timothy's idea."

Abbe's body shook violently, and he stared at Penelope with tear-swollen eyes. "Impossible! You're lying!"

"Don't you know? Timothy was a palace official, the Palace Manager. Queen Owen sent him to Sunder, where he served as a military inspector under the King of Nixie. He infiltrated Sabra Village as a spy. If you don't believe me, send someone to Poiema to verify."

"King of Nixie... spy..." Abbe felt as if a lightning bolt had struck his mind, memories flashing rapidly.

The true identity never revealed to outsiders.

The suggestion to rely on the King of Nixie for supplies.

And Lucas's warning, "One day, we might not fall to the enemy, but to one of our own."

With these thoughts, Abbe nearly fainted. Adam quickly supported him, saying, "Chief Master! Stay strong! Penelope is deceitful, don't believe him! Alan... Timothy could never be a traitor!"

"Believe what you will." Penelope's smile was wide. "Or come with me and ask him yourself. See who he truly serves."

Timothy shivered awake suddenly.

"What time is it?"

He sat up, finding himself alone in Penelope's tent. There was no sign of Penelope.

He tried to stand, but his head throbbed painfully. He sat dazed for a while, waiting for the hangover to pass before slowly getting up and heading for the door.

As he lifted the tent flap, he saw the downpour. Nearby, someone stood with an umbrella. It appeared to be Penelope.

Ignoring the rain, Timothy rushed out, calling, "Hey! Penelope, why didn't you wake me? What time is it? Isn't it time for the talks?"

Penelope, holding a paper umbrella, stared into the rain silently.

"Hey! Don't ignore me, that's creepy!"

Timothy shook Penelope's shoulder, making him turn slowly, eyes fixed on Timothy. "Brother, I've taken Sabra Village for you."

"What?" Timothy was confused. "Abbe agreed to a truce? You've reconciled?"

Penelope's smile was ambiguous. "You drank too much yesterday. Seeing you sleep so soundly this morning, I went to River Filat alone."

Timothy clicked his tongue, annoyed. "Drinking at such a crucial time! So Abbe and his men are back in Sabra Village, right? Is he okay? You didn't harm him?"

Penelope nodded, "Yes, he has 'returned.'"

Timothy sighed in relief, "That's good."

"So brother, let's go back." Penelope grabbed Timothy's hand, smiling innocently.

"Um... wait?" Timothy looked at him blankly, "We?"

"Yes, we," Penelope nodded.

"Go back where?" Timothy asked.

"Of course..." Penelope whispered in Timothy's ear, "Back to Rickie."

Chapter Twenty-Five: Turning Against Each Other

On the way back to Rickie, a cloud of suspicion loomed over Timothy's mind. He couldn't understand why someone like Abbe, who cherished Sabra Village so dearly, would agree to leave for Rickie. Had Penelope already convinced Abbe to lead Sabra Village's people to surrender to Sunder's soldiers? If that were true, it would be the best outcome. But no matter how he looked at it, the progress seemed too smooth, almost unbelievable.

It wasn't until he followed Penelope back to Rickie that Timothy finally realized his intuition had, unfortunately, been correct.

Sabra Village had indeed surrendered and was brought back to Rickie almost without a fight, except for two people—Abbe and Adam.

Pavilion Arnold, Penelope's private retreat, was once a private residence built by his father for a favored concubine. Now, it served as the temporary refuge for Abbe and Adam. The so-called temporary refuge was a euphemism, as the place was heavily guarded by layers of armed soldiers. The doors and windows were all locked with thick chains, making it a luxurious prison.

When Timothy entered the main house of Pavilion Arnold with a nervous heart, what he saw broke his heart.

Tables, chairs, paintings, curtains, plants, and jars—everything that could be destroyed was torn apart. Timothy walked through the mess, slowly approaching the corner where someone was huddled, hugging their knees.

Hearing Timothy's footsteps, the person finally raised their head slowly.

It was Abbe. Timothy looked at those unfocused eyes and thought, but this was no longer the Abbe he knew.

"Master..." Timothy stood in front of Abbe, helpless and dejected, like a child who had done something wrong, hanging his head and not daring to meet Abbe's gaze. "I'm sorry..."

This was clearly not the outcome he wanted. What he wanted was not an Abbe who had been stripped of his soul, leaving only an empty shell.

Abbe's unfocused eyes lingered on Timothy's face for a moment. Suddenly, as if a sharp awl had pierced his brain, he clutched his head, trembling uncontrollably like a frightened beast, and painful whimpers escaped his throat.

"Master!" Timothy was shocked and reached out to hold Abbe, but as soon as he touched him, Abbe reflexively struggled violently, resisting desperately in Timothy's arms.

"Don't be afraid, it's me, Timothy!" Timothy held Abbe's limbs firmly, trying to calm the frightened Abbe.

Seeing that he couldn't break free, Abbe went berserk and bit Timothy's neck hard.

A searing pain tore through Timothy's neck, making his body tense up instantly. Abbe bit down fiercely and hard, and Timothy felt as if a piece of his flesh was about to be torn off. But he gritted his teeth and refused to let go of Abbe, instead holding him even tighter.

If this could slightly alleviate Abbe's pain, Timothy thought, it wouldn't matter even if he actually bit off a piece of flesh.

"...Give him back to me..." Abbe, still biting Timothy's neck, didn't let go even as blood seeped out, and snot and tears soaked into the bloody wound. He whispered through gritted teeth, "Give my uncle back to me..."

As he said this, Abbe finally couldn't hold back and began to cry silently, hugging Timothy. Blood and tears intertwined freely, making his once handsome face a mess.

Timothy felt as if his chest was being torn open. He had learned from the surrendered soldiers of Sabra Village how Lucas died—something he never could have imagined.

If he hadn't been delayed by drinking, if he had arrived in time that day, Lucas wouldn't have had to die.

"I'm sorry..." Although he knew that an apology couldn't bring the dead back to life, Timothy didn't know what else to say.

"So... what Penelope said... it's all true, isn't it?" Abbe, after crying on Timothy's shoulder for a while, spoke softly.

"Penelope?" Timothy was confused, "What did he tell you?"

Abbe's body shook, and suddenly, as if from nowhere, he mustered the strength to push Timothy away. Timothy fell to the ground, staring blankly at him.

Abbe, with bloodshot eyes full of despair and misery, glared at him, "Even now, you want to keep it from me, Timothy?"

Hearing the name "Timothy," his heart sank. He hurriedly got up and said, "Master, you misunderstood, it's not what you think...!"

"Just tell me, yes or no!" Abbe roared.

"...Yes, I am from the palace." Timothy admitted, "But my purpose in coming to Sunder was..."

"Who do you serve!" Abbe interrupted him, staring at him fiercely.

"The Emperor..." Timothy confessed, "I came here to serve the Emperor..."

Before he could finish, there was a loud crash as Abbe split a nearly broken table in half with his palm and swung a broken table leg at Timothy's head.

"Wait!" Timothy, terrified, instinctively dodged, but Abbe quickly pounced on him, pinning him against the wall.

"Master... listen to me!" Timothy tried to awaken Abbe's reason.

"Shut up! Don't call me Master!" Abbe, now a different person, had lost all the tenderness he once had for Timothy. "That dog Emperor killed my entire family and implicated my whole clan. Since you serve him, you're an enemy of the Simpson family!"

Implicated the whole clan? Could it be...

Despite the urgent situation, Timothy's mind inexplicably flashed back to the moment he saw Christopher signing the edict in Hall Zona.

That's right, Queen Owen forced Christopher to execute those two ministers, one was Secretary Robin, the other was Chancellor... Payton!

"Payton... was your father!?" Timothy couldn't believe it. If he hadn't experienced it himself, he wouldn't have believed such a coincidence.

"Don't mention my father's name!!" Abbe raised the broken wood high, aiming it at Timothy's neck. Timothy grabbed the wood.

"Wait! Mas... Abbe! Listen to me! The Emperor didn't kill your family, he was forced!"

But Abbe, completely consumed by rage, couldn't hear Timothy's explanation. As they struggled, a figure suddenly rushed out from the side, knocking the wood out of Abbe's hand.

Penelope stepped forward swiftly, punching Abbe in the stomach, making him spit blood and stagger back.

"Abbe!" Timothy panicked and was about to rush forward but was pulled back by Penelope.

"Don't go! He's lost his mind now." Penelope said coldly, "Guards! Put him in shackles!"

No sooner had he spoken than two guards rushed in, grabbed Abbe's hands, and shackled him with heavy iron cuffs.

"Give my father back! Give my uncle back!"

Abbe struggled in pain, his anguished cries stabbing into Timothy's heart like sharp knives, rendering him speechless.

Was this tear-streaked face really the same as the boy who once smiled at him in the sunset? That pure smile was gone, replaced by endless regret and pain.

Timothy couldn't remember how he left Pavilion Arnold. That day, he was in a daze, as if his soul had left his body. He had only a vague impression of what happened later or what Penelope told him. Only Abbe's last shouted words before he left Pavilion Arnold echoed in his ears like a curse.

The next day, Timothy returned to Pavilion Arnold.

This time, Penelope accompanied him. Hearing that Timothy was still determined to go to Pavilion Arnold, Penelope finally frowned impatiently, but despite his reluctance, he said nothing. After a night of tossing and turning, the more Timothy thought about it, the more he felt there was something fishy about Sabra Village's surrender. He wanted to know what really happened that day on the banks of the River Filat. Now that Abbe had completely lost his mind and was not someone Timothy could communicate with, at least not in the short term, Timothy couldn't bear to provoke him further. So today, Timothy sought out Adam, who was also confined at Pavilion Arnold.

Unlike Abbe, who was held in the main house, Adam was imprisoned in a somewhat secluded attic.

Timothy brushed off Penelope and went upstairs alone, finding Adam sitting on a cushion in front of a statue, his eyes closed and lips moving slightly, as if in silent prayer.

"Adam..."

Hearing Timothy's voice, Adam was startled and turned his head.

In the instant Adam turned, Timothy saw a flicker of joy in his eyes, but it quickly faded, replaced by doubt, sorrow, and finally anger.

He stood up abruptly, lips tightly pressed, and looked at Timothy with a complex expression.

"Adam, are you... alright?" Timothy asked cautiously, "Are you hurt?"

Adam was silent for a long time before finally shaking his head. "No."

Noticing that Adam seemed to retain some calm and reason, Timothy felt a glimmer of relief and continued, "Yesterday, I went to see Chief Master. He's... not doing well. Seeing him like that, I felt terrible. I never imagined things would turn out this way!"

As he spoke, Timothy took a step forward and tightly grasped Adam's hand.

Adam flinched and couldn't help but take a step back.

"Adam, what happened on the day of the negotiations? Wasn't there supposed to be a truce and withdrawal? Why did uncle fall into an ambush and die?"

Adam gritted his teeth. "You shouldn't ask me that. You should ask Penelope. What truce and negotiation? Penelope clearly just wanted to recruit us, but Chief Master refused, and they broke off negotiations, leading to an ambush. If uncle hadn't stepped up to protect Chief Master, he might have..."

Timothy's mind went blank.

Adam turned his head, paused as if to collect himself, then continued, "Penelope also said you are an official of the court, a spy sent by the King of Nixie, and that the so-called negotiation was your plan from the beginning."

"No, no, no!!" Timothy couldn't listen any longer. He grabbed Adam's hand and started to explain, "Adam, you misunderstood!

Yes... I am indeed a court official and indeed the King's inspector, but..."

"You really did deceive us!" Adam shook off Timothy's hand angrily, his eyes reddening with tears welling up. "We trusted you so much!"

"Listen to me!" Timothy said urgently. "Everything I've done has been for one thing: to overthrow Queen Owen!"

"What?" Adam was stunned. "To overthrow Queen Owen?"

Taking a deep breath, Timothy succinctly yet thoroughly recounted his experiences from the time he entered the palace up to joining Sabra Village.

"Adam, you have to believe me! I've told you everything, even things Penelope doesn't know. Yes, I am loyal to the Emperor, but I never intended to harm anyone in Sabra Village. I was only looking for an ally to help me overthrow Queen Owen. She is the one who ordered the extermination of Mr. Simpson's family. To her, the Emperor is nothing more than a walking stamp. So, Abbe and I should be united against a common enemy! But now..."

Timothy sighed deeply, releasing Adam's hand, and said quietly, "Though Sabra Village has surrendered, it's not the way I wanted it to be..."

Adam looked at Timothy's back in silence, his lips pursed. After a long while, he finally spoke, "I don't know who to trust anymore..."

"Adam..." Timothy looked at him sorrowfully.

"It feels like everything changed overnight," Adam said bitterly. "Uncle, who was fine, is gone just like that. The strong, cheerful Chief Master has been utterly broken. The brothers who once swore to share hardships and joys have started to express gratitude to Penelope, accepting recruitment after entering Rickie and seeing the endless delicacies and silver. There is no more

Sabra Village. You were right; some people are born to share hardships but cannot share prosperity. Only now do I truly understand."

After a long, heavy silence, Timothy slowly said, "Adam, come with me."

Adam was stunned and looked at Timothy, puzzled.

"Come back to Poiema with me." Timothy gently took his hand. "I'll prove to you with my actions that everything I said is true."

Adam remained bewildered. "I don't understand what you mean."

"Did you forget? I told you my stay in Sunder was limited. The three-month period is almost up, and then I will return to Poiema." Timothy's eyes grew resolute. "Although the process and method of recruiting Sabra Village were not what I wanted, at least I have the strength to challenge Queen Owen. I must return to Poiema to save the Emperor. If you don't believe what I said, then stay by my side and watch everything unfold."

Adam looked at Timothy with a complicated expression. After a long silence, he said softly, "Let me think about it."

When Timothy walked out of Pavilion Arnold, Penelope was still standing under a willow tree by the carriage, waiting for him. The gentle breeze made his ornate clothes, usually so pristine, catch a bit of dust.

Timothy walked slowly toward him, trying hard to control his emotions, and said quietly, "Don't you have anything to say to me?"

Penelope looked up, meeting Timothy's sharp gaze without fear, and said firmly, "No."

Before he could finish his sentence, Timothy raised his hand and slapped Penelope hard across the face.

Penelope hadn't expected Timothy to hit him so suddenly, and the slap left him stunned. The guards behind Penelope, shocked by Timothy's audacity, immediately stepped forward, drawing their swords with a swift motion.

"Stop!" Penelope raised a hand to stop the guards, his eyebrows raised defiantly. "Let him hit me! If it makes him feel better."

Timothy said nothing and raised his hand again, this time slapping himself hard across the face. This slap was even harder than the one he gave Penelope, splitting his lip and making blood trickle out.

Penelope was taken aback. Timothy's action was completely unexpected.

"These two slaps are for uncle and Abbe."

Timothy glared at Penelope, his eyes burning with anger, and spoke each word deliberately. His usually casual face was now unprecedentedly serious.

After leaving this statement, Timothy didn't look back and walked away quickly.

Penelope watched Timothy's receding figure, his eyes welling up. An indescribable sense of frustration surged within him, and he clutched his chest, feeling as if all his strength had been drained, leaning weakly against the tree trunk, gasping for breath.

"Why did you do that?" A familiar voice came from behind. Penelope turned to see the King of Nixie standing there, looking at him with a complex expression.

"I don't understand what you're talking about." Penelope tried to appear calm.

"Penelope, you're usually so adept at handling people. Don't you know how to win over Abbe? We're all in the same boat. How will we get along if you let things get this tense?" The King of Nixie walked up, pulling a handkerchief from his pocket and handing it to Penelope. "Wipe your eyes. If people see our proud little marquis crying over a man, you'll be a laughingstock."

"I just got something in my eye!" Penelope turned away and quickly wiped his eyes with his sleeve.

The King of Nixie smiled helplessly. "You did wrong, yet you stubbornly refuse to admit it to Timothy. You deserve that slap."

Penelope, now calmer, turned back, his eyes stubbornly defiant. "I'd rather take a hit than back down!"

With that, he turned and walked away quickly.

The King of Nixie had nothing to say. Watching Penelope's retreating figure, he sighed deeply.

Chapter Twenty-Six: Cunningly Provoking Penelope

Despite the various dissatisfactions, Sabra Village—the so-called strongest bandit force in Sunder and Penelope's long-standing concern—was finally officially incorporated.

However, this did not mean that things would be smooth sailing from here on out. The real trouble was just beginning.

Since the people of Sabra Village were essentially a group of un-educated vagrants, years of poverty had ingrained a deep-rooted banditry in them. Instead of reforming after finding a better life, they became more arrogant with a little money. Ever since their incorporation, the Sabra Village members indulged in eating, drinking, whoring, and gambling in Mervyn, committing all kinds of evil. Even the abduction of women in broad daylight occurred from time to time, making their misdeeds notorious.

When Timothy heard these complaints from the King of Nixie, he was not at all surprised. Thinking back to the actions of Beard and Dunn Slave when he was imprisoned in the Sabra Village dungeon, he knew how terrifying an unchecked Sabra Village could be. Back then, with Abbe, Adam, and Lucas still around, they could barely keep the rabble in check. Now that those who could control them were gone, it was no surprise they would run rampant.

The question was, who would manage this group? Or rather, who could control them?

Penelope was out of the question. At the mention of Sabra Village, Penelope showed nothing but disdain, calling them scum and riffraff. There was no way he would personally manage them, and he refused to set foot in their barracks, as if staying there would bring bad luck.

It seemed that Timothy would have to take matters into his own hands.

The reason the Sabra Village members were so unruly was, frankly, a lack of a strict reward and punishment system. Timothy pondered this day and night for several days, using all his knowledge to draft twenty-four military regulations. These regulations covered everything from daily life to marching, training, and fighting, with detailed rules and clear rewards and punishments.

After completing this work, Timothy revised it multiple times until he was very satisfied. He then presented this proud creation to the King of Nixie for review.

"Simply flawless!" The King of Nixie praised it after reading, then turned the conversation. "But Sabra Village is now part of Sunder's army and no longer under my jurisdiction. You should present this to Penelope."

Timothy frowned and clicked his tongue. "But I don't want to go to Morris, that's why I came to you."

The King of Nixie patted Timothy's shoulder with a wry smile. "It's been ten days, and you're still sulking?"

Indeed, ten days had passed since their last unhappy parting. During these days, Timothy and Penelope hadn't seen each other or spoken. It wasn't that Timothy deliberately avoided Penelope; he had his own residence and only needed to report to the King of Nixie for his activities, so their paths rarely crossed.

The thought of facing that sly, sarcastic person again exhausted Timothy.

"I want to know where he is." Timothy sighed. "But he's been elusive these days, and I haven't seen a trace of him."

"You can find him at Esben," the King of Nixie winked. "I've heard Penelope has been staying there recently."

"Esben?" Timothy asked curiously. "What kind of place is that?"

The King of Nixie didn't answer, leaving only a mysterious smile. When Timothy arrived at Esben with the military regulations and saw Penelope surrounded by courtesans, he finally understood the meaning behind the King of Nixie's smile.

The name Esben sounded elegant, but it was actually a brothel. It not only had women but also men and catered only to officials of the fifth rank or above, making it a high-class establishment.

Even surrounded by such a charming group, Penelope didn't seem particularly happy. He absentmindedly listened to the music, drinking sullenly, and didn't notice Timothy's arrival. His eyes were fixed on the void, deep in thought.

It wasn't until Timothy couldn't help but cough that Penelope's gaze returned.

"What a rare guest," Penelope said, clearly surprised by Timothy's presence. "I didn't expect Mr. Shaw to come to such a place."

"Mr. Morris, you're joking. I can't afford to come here," Timothy waved the military regulations in his hand. "If it weren't for the King of Nixie telling me to find you here, I wouldn't even have heard of Esben. But Mr. Morris, no matter how much you enjoy yourself, you shouldn't treat this place as your home, right?"

Although Timothy was an inspector, he had no real power and was far below Penelope in rank. Someone as proud as Penelope would have already thrown out anyone else who spoke to him this way. But for some reason, Timothy's words didn't anger Penelope. He just waved off the courtesans around him.

"I can go wherever I please. Who are you to control me?" Penelope glanced lazily at Timothy.

"A dignified provincial official, spending all day on pleasure without doing any serious work. If this gets out, I don't care, but it's Mr. Morris's own reputation at stake."

"Reputation is just an external matter. I didn't realize, brother, you're so mundane." Penelope smiled mockingly.

Timothy shrugged nonchalantly. "Yes, I'm as mundane as they come, completely unlike you, Mr. Morris, an 'immortal' untouched by worldly matters. Didn't you know?"

These words seemed to hit a nerve. Penelope stood up abruptly, his expression darkening, almost losing his temper but restraining himself at the last moment.

"What do you want? If you're here just to irritate me, you can leave now."

Timothy handed him the scroll of military regulations. "These are the twenty-four military rules I drafted to discipline Sabra Village. Please review them."

Penelope, clearly displeased with Timothy's attitude, clicked his tongue and snatched the scroll from his hand.

"Unexpectedly, you have some knowledge," Penelope said, skimming through the scroll. After reading it thoroughly, he tossed it back to Timothy. "Rewrite it."

Timothy was puzzled. "Why?"

"Isn't it obvious?" Penelope glanced at him. "How many of those ruffians from Sabra Village can read? You wrote it so eloquently, are you planning to cast pearls before swine?"

"That's true... so what should I do?" Timothy frowned at the scroll.

"That's simple. If they can't read, they can at least understand pictures, right?"

"But I'm terrible at drawing, worse than writing..."

"If you want to slack off, just say so." Penelope didn't believe him. He clapped his hands, calling for ink and paper. "Draw here and let me see how bad it can be."

"What should I draw?"

"Anything."

"Anything at all?"

"Just draw, stop with the nonsense." Penelope clicked his tongue impatiently.

Timothy, at a loss for what to draw, hesitated for a long while, his eyes rolling several times before finally settling on Penelope's face.

Feeling Timothy's unwavering gaze, Penelope awkwardly turned his face away, covering it slightly with his fan.

"I told you to draw, why are you staring at me?" Penelope's tone was slightly annoyed.

Suddenly inspired, Timothy shouted, "I've got it!" and began sketching quickly. The result was a grotesque figure that looked neither like a dog nor a pig, impossible to describe.

"What are you drawing?" Penelope frowned, puzzled. "A pig's head?"

"It's you," Timothy explained, pointing at the drawing. "Look, these are the eyes, the nose, the mouth. And this, this is your favorite fan."

"Timothy!" Penelope could no longer contain his anger. He drew his sword with a loud clang. "You're looking for death!"

"I told you my drawing is terrible, but you didn't believe me." Timothy, unfazed, calmly pressed the sword back into its sheath, looking innocent. "Besides, you're the one who called it a pig's head, not me."

Penelope was speechless with rage. He snatched the pen from Timothy's hand, quickly drawing on the paper. In no time, lively little figures filled the sheet. Timothy was amazed and moved closer to watch Penelope's rapid strokes. Before long, the picture was complete, illustrating the military regulations vividly.

"Like this. Do you understand?" Penelope tossed the brush aside, raising his eyebrows.

Timothy applauded in amazement. "Mr. Morris, your artistic skills are remarkable. Such talent shouldn't go to waste. Why don't you illustrate all twenty-four rules yourself?"

"You...!"

Penelope realized he had fallen into Timothy's trap. His face changed, ready to explode, but Timothy didn't give him the chance. Shouting, "Mr. Morris, please continue enjoying yourself! I must take my leave!" he slipped away, vanishing in an instant.

"Timothy... you stop right there!!" Penelope chased out of Esben, clutching the military regulations, but the bustling street revealed no trace of Timothy.

Realizing he had once again lost to Timothy, Penelope almost tore the regulations in fury. He stared at the drawing, feeling as if the pig's head was mockingly grinning at him.

"This doesn't look like me at all; it looks like you..." Penelope muttered, holding back his anger. He put the regulations into his sleeve and left in a hurry.

Timothy's provocation worked. After ten days of slacking, Penelope finally took action. Not only did he illustrate the twenty-four military regulations, but he also rewrote Timothy's text into simple rhymes, had them copied, and distributed to ensure everyone in Sabra Village had a copy.

Penelope required everyone to memorize the regulations and had Timothy check daily. Those who could recite them were rewarded; those who couldn't were punished. Any violators of the military rules would be dealt with according to military law.

The implementation of these twenty-four regulations quickly spread throughout Nuri Camp, curbing the soldiers' bad habits. However, as the saying goes, a leopard can't change its spots. Some disregarded the rules and continued their ways, resulting in a significant incident.

This time, the troublemakers were the most unruly soldiers in Nuri. These four or five men, habitual freeloaders, got drunk in a tavern in Mervyn, not only wrecking the place but also assaulting the tavern keeper's wife and daughter.

By an unfortunate coincidence, the tavern keeper was a distant relative of Penelope. He tearfully demanded justice from Penelope, who frequented the tavern himself. Outraged, Penelope broke his rule of not entering Nuri Camp. In front of hundreds of soldiers, he dragged out the offenders, gave each a hundred lashes, and had their manhood cut off and forced into their mouths.

That day, Nuri Camp resembled a hellish scene, filled with screams and pleas for mercy. Even the hardened bandits of Sabra Village were terrified, stunned into silence.

The effect of this brutal example was immediate. After witnessing Penelope's ruthlessness, the Sabra Village soldiers dared not misbehave in Mervyn again, and the military discipline improved drastically.

When Adam heard this from Timothy, he shuddered. "That's too cruel..."

"This is called fighting fire with fire. Those scoundrels had it coming, meeting Penelope's wrath. I don't pity them at all," Timothy said.

"Those men deserved their fate," Adam muttered. "I just realized how dangerous it was to oppose someone like Penelope. He may look good, but appearances are deceiving."

"Don't be fooled by his looks, or you'll end up like me." Timothy's tone shifted. "What worries me is you, Adam..."

"Me?" Adam was puzzled.

"Take me, for example. I thought I was smart, but I kept falling for Morris's tricks. You're kind and good-hearted. If you meet someone like Penelope, you might not survive."

"Has Penelope bullied you again?" Adam's concern flared up.

"It's not what you think..." Timothy smiled wryly. "I'm worried about you."

"But I can protect myself." Adam's eyes widened, raising his fists. "If Penelope dares bully you again, I'll teach him a lesson! ...But, I'm still not free, so I can't..."

"Adam..." Timothy's heart warmed. "I appreciate your concern, but nothing matters more to me than you and Abbe being safe."

At the mention of Abbe, Adam's expression darkened, his eyes lowered.

"I always knew Penelope was formidable, but now I see the gap between us. No wonder Chief Master, uncle, and I together couldn't defeat him. How is Chief Master now?"

Timothy was silent for a long time, gazing at the drizzling rain outside the window. "He's not eating and has lost a lot of weight."

"Uncle's death hit him hard," Adam said sadly.

"Watching him grow weaker each day hurts me too," Timothy turned back. "Adam, can you suggest something to improve Abbe's appetite? Is there anything he particularly likes to eat?"

"Something he likes...?" Adam tilted his head in thought. "Chief Master never cared much about food. If I must say, perhaps green plums?"

"Green plums?" Timothy was surprised by the answer.

"Chief Master told me this story. As a mischievous child, he hated studying at home. Once, he played outside all day and was caught by his father, who nearly beat him to death. Uncle couldn't stand it and secretly gave him a plum. The sourness made him forget the pain."

"So, he grew to love green plums?"

Adam shook his head. "I can't say for sure, but he remembered it fondly. Chief Master said his taste was naturally dull, often unable to tell good food from bad. But for some reason, that plum stayed in his mind for years."

"Unforgettable..." Timothy stared at the rain, imagining young Abbe biting into a plum, shivering from the sourness, and then laughing.

Perhaps people are the same. Once love or memory enters the heart, it's hard to forget.

Chapter Twenty-Seven: The Young Phoenix's Pure Voice

In early summer, when the branches were lush and green, the green plums were beginning to form.

The belated drizzle had fallen over Sunder for three days, and the scent of fresh grass mixed with the earthy smell of wet soil pervaded Pavilion Arnold, giving the air a dampness that seemed tangible, as if one could wring water from it with a squeeze.

On this day, like every day, Timothy arrived at Pavilion Arnold with a food box, first going to the attic to chat with Adam before heading downstairs to the main house.

This had become Timothy's daily ritual. He knew Abbe didn't want to see him and that the meals he brought were often ignored, ending up in Timothy's own stomach. Yet, he persevered, bringing food daily without fail.

Abbe had lost a lot of weight. He wasn't intentionally starving himself, but his appetite was poor, and even when he ate, he often vomited most of it out. Once, he vomited so severely that he brought up bile, which scared Timothy into thinking he had been poisoned. A doctor confirmed it was not poison but the result of prolonged mental and emotional exhaustion.

After half a month of this ordeal, Abbe's once handsome face had turned pale with a sickly greenish tinge. Thin skin stretched over delicate veins, and his emaciated body seemed so fragile it might break with a light touch. There was no trace of his former fierce vigor.

On this day, as usual, Abbe was sitting by the window, staring blankly outside like a caged bird. Timothy knew Abbe didn't want to interact with him, so he quietly approached, setting the food box on the table beside him.

Today, Timothy had added a dried plum to the meal, hoping Abbe might like it. After leaving, Timothy didn't depart immediately but hid around the corner, nervously observing Abbe's reaction.

Not long after Timothy left, Abbe turned to look at the food box, noticing a note on top. He picked it up and read: "Don't throw it away. You'll like it."

Abbe's hand froze in mid-air for a moment before he finally opened the food box.

As usual, it contained a meticulously prepared, delicious meal. But this time, nestled in the white rice was a single dried plum.

Abbe's eyes widened slightly.

Timothy, hiding outside the window, watched anxiously. Abbe stared at the plum for a long time before finally picking it up and taking a small bite.

Time seemed to stop at that moment. Abbe stood still, and after a long while, a single tear silently slid down his cheek.

Seeing this, Timothy felt a sharp pang in his chest.

That day, for the first time since being confined to Pavilion Arnold, Abbe finished all the food in the box. It was a significant milestone, and Timothy believed his "plum strategy" had worked. From then on, Abbe gradually regained his appetite. He no longer merely nibbled at the meals or ignored them but ate them entirely. Though he still ignored Timothy, showing no sign of acknowledgment, Timothy didn't mind. Seeing Abbe's health improve day by day lightened his heart considerably.

As a result, a dried plum became a daily necessity in each meal. The story of Timothy picking green plums every day eventually reached the King of Nixie's ears. Initially puzzled, the King inquired and learned the whole story. Upon discovering that Abbe was Payton's orphan, the King of Nixie was taken aback and insisted on accompanying Timothy to Pavilion Arnold to visit Abbe.

Abbe had grown accustomed to Timothy's visits, but he was surprised to see the King of Nixie with him this time.

"Who are you?!" Abbe demanded, bristling like a cat encountering a stranger, his eyes full of wariness.

"I am the King of Nixie," the King of Nixie replied calmly. "I had met your father, Payton, several times."

"My father...?" Abbe looked at the King of Nixie in disbelief.

"Perhaps you won't believe me," the King of Nixie said, pulling out half of a jade pendant from his pocket and handing it to Abbe. "But seeing this, Mr. Simpson should have some impression."

Abbe took the half pendant and, upon examining it, trembled all over.

Engraved on the pendant were the characters "Young Phoenix."

"This is... the half pendant my father lost!" Abbe exclaimed, staring at the King of Nixie. "How did it end up in your possession?"

The King of Nixie smiled slightly. "Your father gave it to me."

"Impossible!" Abbe was incredulous. "This pendant is a family heirloom of the Simpson family, with the words 'Young Phoenix Pure Voice' engraved on it. My father cherished it and would never give it away."

"Cherished indeed..." The King of Nixie gazed at the pendant, a nostalgic look in his eyes, as he began to recount the story. "Back then, I was still in Poiema, and your father, Mr. Simpson, was the Chancellor. Mr. Simpson was a principled man who couldn't tolerate corruption, always opposing the faction of Queen Owen. One day, after a court debate, Mr. Simpson had an altercation with Bowie. During the scuffle, the pendant fell and broke.

Strangely, only one half, inscribed with 'Pure Voice,' was found, while the other half disappeared."

Timothy, who had been silently listening, was intrigued. "Could it have been stolen by that Butler?"

The King of Nixie nodded. "Besides Mr. Simpson, the only other person present was Bowie. Naturally, the missing half fell into Bowie's hands."

"But why would he do that?" Abbe asked, puzzled.

"Taking someone's token without reason is usually to frame them," Timothy interjected.

The King of Nixie sighed. "Mr. Shaw is correct. I was unaware of this until one day, while playing chess with the Emperor in the palace garden, a concubine rushed in, claiming Bowie had forced her to use the pendant to frame Mr. Simpson for an affair. She presented the pendant to the Emperor."

That concubine was smart, realizing that colluding with Bowie would only bring disaster, so she betrayed him.

Timothy was surprised to learn that Christopher was involved in this incident.

"But the Emperor was under Queen Owen's control. He couldn't have made a decision on this matter, right?" Timothy couldn't help but ask.

"Exactly," the King of Nixie nodded. "Seeing the Emperor's difficulty, I took the pendant. The Emperor then dismissed the concubine from the palace under a pretext."

"And then?" Abbe pressed.

"Bowie's plot failed, so he had to abandon it. Later, I found Mr. Simpson and returned the pendant, but he refused to take it back and instead gave it to me in gratitude for saving him."

"So that's how it was..." Abbe was silent, clutching the half pendant with the characters "Young Phoenix" tightly, unable to speak.

"I never expected that within six months of my departure from Poiema, the Simpson family would suffer such a calamity..."

Timothy couldn't help but feel a pang of regret. It seemed the conflict between Bowie and Payton had deep roots. Bowie had long wanted to remove Payton but had no opportunity due to the King of Nixie. After the King of Nixie was ousted from Poiema for protecting the Crown Prince, Payton lost his shield and fell victim to Bowie's machinations.

"Your Highness," Abbe knelt before the King of Nixie. "I didn't recognize the great benefactor of my family. I thank you on behalf of my father."

With that, he bowed his head to the ground.

The King of Nixie quickly helped him up. "Good child, knowing you are alive is a great comfort to me. Tell me, how did you survive the disaster that befell your family?"

"I was not in Poiema when it happened, so I escaped. Later, thanks to my uncle's protection, I fled back to Sunder and have survived until now."

The King of Nixie nodded understandingly, his expression heavy as he gently patted Abbe on the head, speaking softly, "Child, mourn and move on. The dead cannot be revived. If your father and uncle were still alive, they would certainly want you to live well."

(Abbe, you must live... live well...)

Lucas's last words echoed faintly in his ears, and Abbe's heart ached as tears fell like raindrops.

Timothy moved closer, gently taking Abbe's hand and slipping a green plum into his palm.

Abbe was startled, slowly lifting his tear-filled eyes to look into Timothy's somber gaze, which held an indescribable emotion.

Seeing that Abbe did not pull away, Timothy mustered his courage and placed his other hand over Abbe's.

"You still have us," Timothy said, looking into Abbe's eyes.

At first, there were soft gasps, then gradually, the sobs grew louder until Abbe could no longer hold back and began to cry openly. Timothy pulled Abbe into his arms, holding him tightly, letting Abbe bury his face in his chest and weep uncontrollably. He hoped these tears would wash away the dark clouds hanging over Abbe's heart and restore the boyish smile like spring sunshine.

That night, Timothy had a dream. In the dream, he and Abbe sat side by side at the door, Abbe holding a food box in one hand and a green plum in the other, eating contentedly. Timothy watched Abbe's blissful expression with envy and curiosity. "Is that plum really so delicious?"

"Do you want to try?" Abbe asked, looking at him with bright eyes, a bite of the plum in his mouth.

"Yes..."

Timothy nodded, and before he could finish speaking, Abbe unexpectedly pressed his soft lips to his. Their tongues intertwined, sharing a tangy sweetness that was both tart and delightful.

Unfortunately, the dream was too short. Just as it reached the most crucial moment, dream Abbe vanished like a phantom, leaving Timothy with a sense of longing and regret.

If possible, Timothy wished to spend more time unraveling Abbe's emotional knots, but time waited for no one. As the three-month period drew nearer, Timothy's feelings grew increasingly conflicted.

He couldn't bear to leave Abbe, but thoughts of Christopher also weighed heavily on his mind. Two months had passed since Timothy sent his last letter, and neither he nor the King of Nixie had heard from Poiema since. Whether Christopher had received his letter, how he was doing, and what had happened in the palace were all unknown to Timothy.

Both Sunder and Poiema held people and matters Timothy could not abandon, something he hadn't anticipated three months ago.

But what Timothy didn't expect even more was that he wasn't the only one eagerly awaiting news. Christopher, far away in Poiema, was just as anxious.

A week after Timothy left Poiema, Christopher wrote a letter and had it sent to Sunder. From that day on, he waited eagerly, day and night, but Timothy's reply never came.

Was Timothy too busy? Or was there another reason? Christopher didn't dare to speculate.

All he could do was wait, in the vast and lonely palace—

The moonlight was serene, and the cicadas sang endlessly. In the heavily curtained Hall Zona, muffled, lascivious moans echoed.

"Ah... Timothy..."

On the dragon bed, Christopher's body lay bare, his breath heavy. Between his spread legs was a lifelike dildo, moving in and out of his wet hole.

This wasn't the first time Christopher had used this toy. Ever since Timothy left Poiema, Christopher had been unbearably lonely. Now, without Timothy's letters, he had nothing to cling to and could only seek solace in the toy each night.

The toy was truly remarkable, not only resembling the real thing but also capable of expanding. As Christopher used it, it would swell to fill him completely, the sensation akin to being nibbled by a thousand ants, both numbing and intensely arousing.

"Timothy... Timothy..."

Lost in self-pleasure, Christopher's voice grew more uninhibited. He moaned Timothy's name repeatedly, his lips parted, his breath quickening.

Despite the cool summer breeze in Poiema, Christopher's forehead, cheeks, and body were flushed with desire, beads of sweat forming on his skin.

"Ah..."

Christopher closed his eyes, imagining Timothy smiling roguishly at him. It felt as if Timothy, not the toy, was inside him. This thought made his mouth dry, and his bare feet rubbed restlessly against the blanket. He couldn't help but quicken his pace, thrusting the toy in and out more forcefully. After hundreds of strokes, his abdomen tightened, and a wave of pleasure surged through him. He cried out, mindlessly pushing the toy deeper as his hips lifted off the bed, climaxing in spasms that sent jets of white fluid out.

Trembling, Christopher felt like he had lost his soul, staring blankly at the night sky outside the window.

In the endless longing and melancholy, Christopher passed yet another ordinary, yet utterly dull night. This brief, secret pleasure should have been just another insignificant page in his monotonous life.

But Christopher had no idea that this seemingly unnoticed secret had sown the seeds of danger.

Chapter Twenty-Eight: Unresolved Enemies

The next day, Christopher returned to Hall Zona after court in his imperial sedan. As he approached the entrance, he saw a figure standing outside.

"Urijah Rogers, greetings to the Emperor."

The man bowed to Christopher, then raised his head.

This person was tall, with a fair face and red lips, strikingly handsome, yet there was a touch of seductiveness in his movements. Christopher stared at him for a moment, unable to recall who he was, until a eunuch whispered a reminder in his ear: "Mr. Rogers is a trusted aide of Queen Owen."

The eunuch emphasized "trusted aide," which was a polite way of saying that Urijah was Queen Owen's lover. Christopher immediately understood and did not wish to engage further with Queen Owen's people. He responded indifferently, "What is it?"

"I have something I wish to present to Your Majesty."

"What is it?"

Urijah looked uneasy. "This item is extremely private. It would be inappropriate to discuss it here with so many people around..."

A private matter? Christopher eyed Urijah suspiciously, then said in a low voice, "Follow me."

Christopher led Urijah into Hall Zona, dismissing his attendants to wait outside the hall, then turned to Urijah.

"Now, what is it?"

Seeing they were alone, Urijah's demeanor changed. He smirked and said, "Your Majesty, yesterday while organizing documents in the Imperial Household Department, I found a letter mixed among the files. It was unsigned, so I opened it, and what a discovery it was! Shall I read it to you?"

Urijah pulled a letter from his sleeve and began to read aloud.

"Seeing your letter is like seeing you. I have received your letter. All is well in Sunder, and the task you entrusted to me is progressing smoothly. As the days pass, so does my longing for you. I hope to finish everything soon and return to you."

From the first word, Christopher's face turned pale. As Urijah continued, Christopher's hands and feet grew cold, and he began to tremble.

"Stop reading!" Christopher shouted, ignoring the usual decorum, and lunged for the letter. "Give it back to me!"

But Urijah sidestepped nimbly, holding the letter out of reach. "As I read this passionate letter, I couldn't help but wonder who wrote it to Your Majesty. Upon reflection, I remembered that the inspector sent to Sunder was Timothy—Timothy, wasn't it?"

Christopher felt his blood run cold, but he forced himself to remain calm. "So what if it is?"

"I just find it puzzling. Your Majesty and Timothy hardly interacted before. When did this deep relationship start? But honestly, it's none of my business who Your Majesty befriends. So last night, I thought I'd secretly return the letter to you, but then..."

Christopher's mind went blank as Urijah chuckled and leaned in to whisper in his ear, "I heard some very interesting sounds."

Christopher's face changed colors, red and white, as he lowered his head, biting his lip, avoiding Urijah's gaze.

Urijah, unrestrained and arrogant, was Queen Owen's favorite. Emboldened by her favor, he had long since ceased to regard Christopher as his superior. Seeing Christopher's unease, Urijah became even more brazen, reaching out a finger to lift Christopher's chin.

"Who knew, a man can be even more wanton than a woman."

Christopher recoiled in disgust, slapping Urijah's hand away. "How dare you! Get out!"

"Oh? You want me to leave?" Urijah saw through Christopher's bluff. He leisurely waved the letter. "Fine, I'll take this to Queen Owen and tell her every detail of what I saw and heard last night. How does that sound?"

Christopher felt faint with anger and fear. As Urijah turned to leave, he rushed forward, blocking his way.

"Don't go!" Christopher's voice trembled. "What do you want? As long as you keep this secret, I'll agree to anything!"

Urijah smiled triumphantly. "Anything?"

Christopher bit his lip until it turned white, closing his eyes in despair as Urijah approached, trapping his wrists against the door.

Just then, urgent knocking on the door interrupted them.

"Your Majesty! Are you inside?"

It was Arya's voice!

Christopher shouted, "Arya! I'm here!"

Urijah frowned, clicking his tongue in annoyance, and reluctantly released Christopher's hands. In a moment, the door was flung open, and Arya rushed in, glaring at Urijah before turning to Christopher, who sat pale and trembling.

"Arya!" Tears welled in Christopher's eyes. Arya glared at Urijah again before kneeling in front of Christopher. "Your Majesty, are you alright?"

"I feel dizzy," Christopher murmured.

Arya held Christopher's hand, examining his face. "You may have caught a chill. You should rest." He then turned to Urijah. "Mr. Rogers, the Emperor is unwell. Do you have any other business?"

Urijah, frustrated by this interruption, reluctantly replied, "Just don't forget what you promised, Your Majesty."

With a bow, he left quietly.

Once Urijah was gone, Christopher let out a long sigh of relief. Arya wasted no time inquiring about the situation, and Christopher, trusting Arya's loyalty, recounted Urijah's blackmail.

Arya listened and then said quietly, "Your Majesty, you must stop writing letters to Timothy."

Christopher nodded silently, knowing Arya was right. The best way to avoid suspicion was to do nothing. The palace was full of spies, especially Queen Owen's, and Urijah's actions were a stark reminder of the dangers.

"But what if Urijah uses this against me again?" The thought of Urijah's earlier advances made Christopher nauseous.

"I have a solution," Arya said, his gaze steady.

Christopher perked up. "What is it? Tell me!"

"Urijah is known for his debauchery. Though he is Queen Owen's favorite, he is infamous for his indiscretions, pursuing both men and women," Arya said disdainfully.

Christopher was shocked. "Does Queen Owen know this?"

Arya shook his head. "Given her suspicious nature, if she knew, she wouldn't tolerate it."

Like a lightning bolt, realization struck Christopher. He met Arya's cold gaze, understanding immediately.

"This man... cannot be allowed to stay," Christopher muttered to himself.

Within days, rumors of Urijah's promiscuity spread like wildfire throughout the palace.

When Queen Owen heard, she was furious. Normally, such betrayal would result in immediate execution. However, Urijah's family ties to Bowie, Queen Owen's nephew, complicated matters. Bowie pleaded for his friend, and Queen Owen, for her nephew's sake, spared Urijah's life, stripping him of his title and banishing him to Mausoleum Rudolf, ending the scandal quietly.

Christopher felt a sense of relief. The danger had passed for now, but he dared not write to Timothy again.

As for Urijah, his scandalous behavior continued in Mausoleum Rudolf, where his debauchery eventually led to his downfall. But that is another story.

Meanwhile, in Sunder, the three-month period had quickly come to an end, and just before returning to Poiema, Timothy received some exciting news—Adam had finally agreed to accompany him to Poiema.

With Adam's agreement, Timothy felt a great sense of relief. Although Adam insisted that he was only going to keep an eye on Timothy for the Chief Master, Timothy knew that Adam's willingness to return to Poiema with him indicated his trust.

However, when Timothy took Adam's hand and brought him before Penelope, requesting permission to take Adam with him, Penelope narrowed his eyes and scrutinized Adam from head to toe for a long time before finally giving a reluctant nod.

The night before their departure, the King of Nixie hosted a farewell banquet in his palace garden for Timothy and Adam. It was Adam's first time at the King of Nixie's residence and his first time interacting with such an important figure. Initially, he was very reserved, speaking in a voice barely above a whisper. However, after a few glasses of warm wine, Adam began to loosen up. Discovering the King of Nixie's cheerful and straightforward nature, and knowing that he was the savior of the Simpson family, Adam soon opened up and started talking more freely.

"Adam, drink less. We have a journey ahead of us tomorrow," Timothy cautioned, noticing the flush on Adam's face and the signs of intoxication. He quickly took the cup from Adam's hand.

The King of Nixie had been observing the two closely. He couldn't help but ask, "I see that Adam looks very young, maybe fifteen or sixteen. Why do you call him brother, Mr. Shaw?"

Adam seemed a bit embarrassed, his eyes slightly reddened. "I am sixteen. In terms of age, I should be two years younger than Alan."

Timothy added, "The Prince might not know, but in Sabra Village, Adam's rank is higher than mine. It's only natural for me to call him brother. Besides, Adam saved my life. When I was in the Sabra Village dungeon, if it weren't for Adam giving me..."

Before Timothy could finish, Adam let out a loud cry and rushed to cover Timothy's mouth.

"Dungeon?" The King of Nixie's curiosity was piqued. "What did Adam give you?"

"Nothing, nothing!" Adam shook his head vigorously, stammering, "We didn't do anything! I mean, Alan is drunk, Your Highness. Don't listen to his nonsense."

"Really? Timothy doesn't look drunk to me. He seems quite clear-headed," came a chilling voice from behind Adam. It was Penelope, whose sudden appearance made Adam shiver.

Timothy turned around to see Penelope, fanning himself lightly, with a sly smile on his face. "Mr. Garcia, among friends, what secrets can't be shared?" Penelope's voice was soft, but his gaze was predatory as he lifted Adam's chin with his fan. "I'm very curious. What kind of life-saving grace does Mr. Shaw owe you?"

Penelope's presence was overwhelming, and his eyes glinted with a cold light that made Adam's skin crawl. Timothy stepped forward, pulling Adam behind him. "What are you up to now? Stay away from Adam!"

Penelope laughed, seemingly pleased with his mischief. "What could I possibly be up to?" he said, a satisfied smile on his face.

"Penelope! You finally showed up!" The King of Nixie greeted Penelope warmly, pulling him to sit beside him. "We've been drinking for a while, and you were nowhere to be seen. I thought you wouldn't come tonight."

"Your Highness jests. How could I not show up for Mr. Shaw's sake? I was delayed because I was preparing a grand farewell gift for Mr. Shaw." Penelope said as he took a seat and downed a full cup of wine.

"A grand gift? Where is it?" The King of Nixie looked around, puzzled.

"If it's a grand gift, it's naturally not something I carry around. It's already been sent to Mr. Shaw's residence."

The King of Nixie was astonished. "A literal 'grand' gift, then? A mountain of gold or silver?"

Penelope laughed, covering his mouth with his fan. "Your Highness, why spoil the surprise? Let Mr. Shaw have his moment of joy."

"Mr. Morris, there's no need for such formality. We're just taking separate paths for now. I'll meet up with you later, so there's no need for a grand farewell." Timothy said calmly.

"That's true." The King of Nixie nodded. "After all, Sunder and Poiema are quite far apart. It's common for there to be no news for a month or two. We need someone to go ahead and scout the situation. Mr. Shaw, with your speed, you'll reach Poiema before us."

"So, tonight is more of an alliance banquet than a farewell?" Penelope raised an eyebrow, looking at both the King of Nixie and Timothy.

"That's one way to put it." The King of Nixie lifted his cup to them. "From today, we are truly one family."

"It's hard to say if we're one family yet." Timothy drank his cup of wine and glanced at Penelope. "I trust His Highness, but I doubt Mr. Morris's loyalty."

Penelope scoffed, about to retort when the King of Nixie grabbed both their hands and clasped them together with his own.

"This venture we're undertaking is extraordinary. If one of us falters, it could lead to our doom and the death of many. We must be united, sharing both joys and sorrows. Penelope, I know you have your schemes. Mr. Shaw, I know you have unresolved issues. But tonight, for my sake, let's put all grievances aside and move forward as brothers."

Timothy couldn't help but laugh at the King of Nixie's heroic tone. "Your Highness, you make it sound like we're forming a sworn brotherhood."

"That's a great idea!" The King of Nixie's eyes lit up, clapping his hands.

"Sworn brotherhood? You must be joking," Penelope rolled his eyes at Timothy. "His Highness is of noble birth, while we are not. It's ridiculous to speak of brotherhood. Besides, haven't we already called each other brothers?"

"And you still stab me in the back?" Timothy taunted.

"Timothy!" Penelope finally snapped, slamming the table. "Are you done yet?"

"Why are you two arguing again..." The King of Nixie rubbed his forehead, noticing Adam watching the two, especially Penelope, with a puzzled expression. He leaned in and whispered, "Adam, they always argue like this. You'll get used to it."

"Is Penelope always like this?" Adam asked.

"Not really." The King of Nixie was surprised by Adam's question. "He's usually quite diplomatic, as long as you don't provoke him. Why do you ask?"

"Nothing." Adam lowered his head, lost in thought as he stared at his cup.

On Timothy's last night before departure, the King of Nixie gave up trying to mediate, allowing Timothy and Penelope to argue freely. Strangely, after a full-blown argument with Penelope, Timothy felt much better. Perhaps it was because he finally had the chance to say everything he had bottled up, releasing all his pent-up frustration.

Timothy considered himself and Penelope as two extremes. Penelope kept too much to himself, while Timothy needed to express his feelings openly to avoid internal strife. There were people in life who became knots in your heart, unresolved and unyielding. Penelope was such a knot for Timothy, an ever-present challenge.

Timothy didn't know if he and Penelope would ever reconcile. That day might never come, but it didn't matter. It was better to be honest and open, even if it meant arguing and fighting, than to harbor hidden resentment.

He only wished to live without regrets and be true to his heart.

Chapter Twenty-Nine: A Great Gift

But then again, what exactly was the "great gift" Penelope mentioned? It couldn't be something so massive that it couldn't be brought over, could it? Perhaps it was truly a room filled with gold and jewels.

With this curious expectation, Timothy nervously pushed open the door to his house.

Red candles flickered, wisps of blue smoke curled in the air, and Timothy's room looked as usual, seemingly unchanged.

"Where is the great gift?"

Timothy was looking around when he suddenly heard a faint moan from behind the heavy drapes. He paused, turned towards the sound, and as a gentle night breeze blew, a vague silhouette was outlined beneath the billowing curtains.

Timothy swallowed hard, reached out, and drew back the layers of curtains, revealing a figure wrapped in a brocade quilt. Beside the quilt was a piece of paper with three large words: "Enjoy Slowly."

"Penelope, what on earth are you up to!?"

Penelope's bizarre behavior left Timothy utterly confused. He quickly stepped forward and lifted the brocade quilt, revealing a person bound tightly with hemp rope, a cloth gag in their mouth, tears of indignation and frustration in their clear eyes, staring wide-eyed at Timothy.

"Abbe!?"

Timothy was dumbfounded. He never expected Abbe to appear before him in such a manner. Stunned for a moment, he quickly came to his senses at Abbe's muffled moans.

"Hold on, I'll untie you right away!"

Timothy bent down to untie the ropes binding Abbe.

"Penelope, you tied a dead knot!" Timothy clicked his tongue in frustration, stood up, and rummaged through the room. Finally, he found a dagger and cut through the ropes restraining Abbe.

After much effort, the ropes were finally undone, and the cloth gag was removed. As soon as Abbe was freed, he kicked Timothy away.

"Don't touch me!"

Abbe's kick hit Timothy squarely in the chest, nearly making him vomit his dinner. Before Timothy could get up, Abbe had already pounced on him, grabbing his collar with one hand and raising the dagger Timothy had used to cut the ropes with the other.

"I knew it! You and Penelope are in this together!" Abbe glared at Timothy, tears of humiliation and anger welling in his eyes.

"Master, you're mistaken. I truly had no idea about this!" Timothy hurriedly defended himself.

"Shut up!" Abbe pressed the dagger to Timothy's throat, gritting his teeth. "You think I don't know you're playing good cop, bad cop? How many times do you plan to pull the same trick on me? Do you take me for a fool, Abbe? Watching me being toyed with makes you happy, doesn't it!?"

Timothy met Abbe's gaze silently.

"Why aren't you saying anything? Feeling guilty because I hit the mark?" Abbe's anger flared, and he pressed the dagger even closer to Timothy's neck. The sharp blade was tight against his pulse, ready to draw blood with any further pressure.

"If killing me will make you feel better, then do it." Timothy looked resigned, adopting an expression of facing death fearlessly.

Abbe froze, apparently not expecting Timothy to give up so suddenly.

But what surprised him even more was that, seeing Abbe's hesitation, Timothy pulled his collar apart, exposing his bare chest unabashedly to Abbe.

Abbe was startled by Timothy's unexpected move, instinctively retreating his hand, only to be grabbed by Timothy, the dagger now pressed against Timothy's left chest.

"Go ahead, strike me right here. For the sake of our master-disciple relationship, give me a quick death." Timothy looked up, meeting Abbe's eyes directly.

Abbe suddenly felt a dryness in his mouth and involuntarily swallowed. Timothy's palm was so hot, like a burning flame, scorching his skin inch by inch. Even the dagger in his hand began to tremble slightly.

Abbe couldn't bring himself to look directly at the person before him, especially that robust, masculine physique, which under the candlelight, exuded a dangerous and alluring aura.

Realizing his breath was becoming increasingly rapid, Abbe anxiously averted his gaze. As his eyes swept over Timothy's lower abdomen, an ugly, jagged scar came into view.

Yes, this was the scar from when Timothy saved him from a knife wound on the hill at Sabra Village.

In an instant, memories flooded back into Abbe's mind.

With a roar, Abbe's eyes filled with resolve. Timothy closed his eyes, accepting his fate, and a sharp chill swept over him, followed by a deadly silence.

When Timothy opened his eyes again, the dagger was embedded in the wall, its blade several inches deep. Abbe, with a look of despair, let go of the handle.

He stood up, staggering a few steps back.

"Master..." Timothy felt a sense of relief, Abbe had softened after all.

Abbe gritted his teeth, turned, and prepared to run away.

"Master, don't go!" Timothy quickly got up and hugged Abbe from behind. His heart raced, and his voice was filled with an uncontrollable excitement and joy. "I knew you couldn't leave me."

"I told you, don't call me Master!" Abbe struggled in Timothy's arms, his voice tinged with sobs. Yet, clearly, his struggles lacked the intensity they had earlier, now carrying a sense of helplessness and timidity.

"Then Abbe!" Timothy's breath grew heavier. "Abbe, you must have feelings for me, otherwise..." Timothy lightly licked Abbe's soft earlobe, "why would you still be wearing the token of love I gave you?"

Abbe shuddered as if electrified, his body turning weak and numb.

"Your ears are still so sensitive, one lick and you go limp," Timothy whispered in Abbe's ear.

"Timothy... you're despicable...!" Abbe protested in a trembling voice.

Although Abbe had his back to Timothy, the bright red of his ears, almost dripping with blood, and the intense heartbeat that could be felt even through his clothes, completely exposed Abbe's insecurity and hesitation. Emboldened, Timothy slid a hand into Abbe's robe, pressing his aroused self against Abbe's buttocks.

"No...!"

Abbe was completely panicked. He shook his head frantically, trying to escape forward, but Timothy's arms held him tightly, leaving him immobile.

"No what? You're clearly aroused too," Timothy said as he slid his hand down to Abbe's crotch, rubbing the swollen object back and forth.

"It's all your fault! It's all because of you...!"

Reluctant to admit that his body responded so easily to Timothy's caresses, Abbe kept shaking his head. Unfortunately, his desire was at odds with his reason. Under Timothy's skilled movements, Abbe's shameful desire reared its head.

Abbe didn't even know when his pants disappeared. When he came to his senses, his thighs were already bare, and his jade stem stood erect between his legs, dripping with dew.

Timothy's long-suppressed desire finally exploded at this moment. He couldn't wait any longer. He grabbed Abbe around the waist and threw him onto the nearby ivory-carved dressing table. Abbe was about to struggle when he suddenly felt a warmth between his legs. Timothy had bent down and taken the erect jade stem into his mouth without warning.

The sudden pleasure was too much for Abbe to handle. His body trembled, and he couldn't help but rub Timothy's cheek with the inside of his bare thigh. One hand feebly pushed at Timothy's head, while the other gripped the edge of the table until his knuckles turned white.

But Timothy wasn't going to let him go easily. He used his tongue to tease, suck, and swallow, each time bringing Abbe to the brink of fainting. At first, Abbe had some strength to struggle, but eventually, he couldn't resist anymore. His legs spread wider and wider, gradually exposing his most private parts to Timothy.

After making the jade stem slick and shiny, Timothy swallowed hard, eagerly spreading the already soaked folds and inserting a finger.

As inexperienced as he was, Abbe couldn't help but let out a gasp at the sudden intrusion. Timothy was both delighted and nervous to finally explore this long-desired forbidden area. He had thought the owner of this place would not welcome him, but as soon as his finger slipped in, the tender walls clung to it like a living thing. After just a few strokes, faint squelching sounds could be heard. Timothy curiously bent his finger and scooped out some saliva and love juice.

No matter how hard Abbe tried to steel his heart, faced with this scene, he was already deeply ashamed, wishing he could smash his head against the dressing table. He covered Timothy's eyes with his hand, trembling, "Don't look..."

But Timothy grabbed his hand, overjoyed. "Abbe, you really do like me."

"I hate you." Abbe lowered his gaze, trembling eyelids covering his eyes, and in the softest voice, he said the harshest words, "I hate you so much I wish I could kill you."

"Then kill me." Timothy couldn't help but embrace him, "Let me die in your arms."

Before Abbe could voice his protest, Timothy's lips sealed his, leading to a fierce entanglement of lips and tongue. Timothy's last ounce of restraint crumbled under this storm of passion. He melted into Timothy's embrace, his legs shyly spreading open, his tender hole already drenched and able to easily swallow three of Timothy's fingers.

Seeing Abbe so moved, Timothy was already rock hard, aching to pull out his shaft and plunge into the place he had dreamt of. "Abbe, I want you."

Even so, Timothy restrained his beastly desire, nearly begging.

Abbe's eyes filled with tears, a mix of emotions swirling, and he whispered, "Since you are so determined, why ask?"

Timothy's chest tightened, his voice heavy, "If you are unwilling, say so now, it's not too late. Otherwise, no matter how much you hit or scold me later, I won't let you go."

Abbe's heart shook. He gazed into Timothy's eyes, seeing the torrent of emotions, and closed his eyes as if bewitched.

Taking this as permission, Timothy wasted no time. He quickly undid his belt, pulling out his throbbing member. Though Abbe's eyes were shut, he could hear Timothy spit into his palm, spreading it on his shaft. His heart raced with nerves.

Timothy grabbed Abbe's knees, spreading his legs wide, pressing his hot, hard tip against Abbe's moist entrance.

"I'm coming in."

Swallowing hard, Timothy guided his thick head to Abbe's tight entrance, teasing it lightly before finally pushing inside.

Abbe's waist trembled as he felt like he was being torn in half. As his body arched back, he let out a muffled cry of pain. Only then did he realize how excruciating it was to be taken by a man.

He used all his strength to resist the intrusion, but Timothy had lost his patience. To prevent Abbe from escaping, he held Abbe's waist tightly, ignoring his futile resistance, and embedded his thick shaft firmly inside him.

"Bastard...!"

Abbe cursed in pain, tears spilling from his eyes. His clenched fists pounded on Timothy's chest, but ultimately, he was no match for Timothy's determined invasion.

"Abbe, relax. You're so tight, I might come too soon."

The moment he entered, Timothy's mind seemed to explode. The searing, wet little hole clung to him like a living thing. If not for holding his breath and gritting his teeth, he might have come right then.

Abbe, inexperienced, knew no tricks. He could only keep pounding Timothy and gasping, "You bastard, bastard, bastard... ah...!"

With a final tremor, it was because Timothy unexpectedly thrust against Abbe's buttocks. Timothy finally managed to take Abbe's body after great effort, and he was not about to let go easily. He instinctively found the most sensitive spot and relentlessly focused on it, thrusting into that tender spot, grinding away with abandon.

Abbe suddenly arched his body, limbs momentarily numb, almost fainting, then awakening amidst waves of tingling sensations. As he opened his eyes, he realized he had lost himself in that moment, staring at the specks of foul-smelling spatter on his lower abdomen, deeply inhaling.

Timothy had never encountered a body as sensitive as Abbe's, as if he had discovered his own secret treasure trove. Excitedly, he lifted Abbe, leaving him completely suspended, then forcefully thrust upward, ravaging that sensitive spot.

The unstable position filled Abbe with fear, fearing he might fall, he clung to Timothy's neck like grasping at a lifeline, enduring the relentless thrusting upon his most vulnerable point.

The quiet of the night amplified the sounds of their passionate union, leaving Abbe feeling both ashamed and helpless. He could only endure as Timothy ravished him repeatedly in this disquieting position, feeling Timothy release inside him, his warm essence flooding in until his insides nearly overflowed.

When finally released, Abbe thought it was over, but before he could catch his breath, Timothy flipped him over against the dressing table and thrust into him again from behind.

Abbe, with slightly dazed eyes, saw his reflection in the mirror, his upper body exposed, his member swaying, droplets of fluids splattering on his sweaty abdomen, some even spattering on the bronze mirror like scattered pearls. The dressing table rattled, and even the curtains beside them swayed in the wind, enhancing the debauchery reflected in the mirror.

"Abbe, even if I were to die on you today, I would have no regrets."

As Timothy continued his vigorous movements, he lifted a sweaty strand of Abbe's hair and gently nibbled on his earlobe, then lowered himself to delicately nibble on it, teasing it with his tongue.

Abbe, overwhelmed by pleasure, his body almost entirely surrendered, continued to curse, "Beast!" Even though even this curse sounded weak, it carried a hint of lasciviousness.

The more defiant Abbe became, the more Timothy's desire surged. In the end, Timothy pinned Abbe against the dressing table, thrusting into him relentlessly.

Because Timothy had already ejaculated once before, Abbe's tender flesh was now moist and slippery, the sound of water flowing with each thrust.

Abbe, though unable to see, felt the tingling sensation replacing the pain, his body itching uncontrollably, his moans carrying a hint of ecstasy.

Just listening to Abbe's melodious moans, Timothy knew Abbe understood the pleasures of lovemaking. This realization further fueled Timothy's desire, making it even harder for him to restrain himself, wishing to thoroughly enjoy this moment of ecstasy. Eventually, even the dressing table seemed unable to withstand Timothy's passion, creaking and swaying under their weight, on the verge of collapse.

That night, they entangled until exhaustion, from the dressing table to the bed, for almost an hour, in a battle of unprecedented intensity, so much so that in the end, even the room filled with incense could not mask the strong odor.

Both Timothy and Abbe were exhausted, especially Abbe, who almost lost all sensation in his limbs. Despite the fatigue, Timothy was satisfied; no matter what, on the last day of leaving Sunder, he finally possessed Abbe—though only physically.

As for Abbe's heart, Timothy believed that one day, it would return to him. He just needed a little more time. Timothy was patient in this regard.

When Abbe woke up again, it was midnight. In a daze, he seemed to hear someone calling his name. But when he opened his tired eyes, all he saw was Timothy, sleeping soundly beside him.

The gentle breeze brought a hint of coolness, typical of a summer night. Abbe quietly sat up, but with a slight movement, he felt a tearing pain below, every joint and muscle in his body protesting, forcing him to face the fact that he had given himself to someone.

Yet, the culprit who had caused all this discomfort was now lying comfortably beside him, blissfully dreaming about something. "Don't run away..." Timothy murmured, as he subconsciously reached out, lazily embracing Abbe's waist. "You're mine..."

Abbe couldn't help but scrutinize the man before him, who made his teeth itch. Post-romance, Timothy's tousled hair, his usual charming eyes, and the cocky tilt of his mouth had all been subdued, revealing a childlike purity and innocence.

"Uncle... What should I do..." Abbe's heart was in turmoil as he reached out, lightly tracing Timothy's masculine cheek with his fingertips.

He admitted he was deluded. Love or hate, in the end, it was an inescapable obsession.

Perhaps unwittingly, he had long been ensnared in the cage called infatuation.